For
Forsyth, C.A.
Katie's Midnight Ride
DISCARD

Katie's Midnight Ride

C. A. Forsyth

James Lorimer & Company, Publishers
Toronto, 1997

James Lorimer & Company Ltd. acknowledges with thanks the support of the Canada Council for the Arts for our publishing program. We also acknowledge the continued support of the federal Department of Canadian Heritage and the Ontario Arts Council in the development of writing and publishing in Canada.

Cover illustration: Ian Watts

Canadian Cataloguing in Publication Data

Forsyth, C.A. (Christine A.)

Katie's midnight ride

(Sports stories)

ISBN 1-55028-575-0 (bound) ISBN 1-55028-574-2 (pbk.)

I. Title. II. Series: Sports stories (Toronto, Ont.)

PS8561.0698K37 1997 jC813'.54C97-930947-6
PZ7.F67Ka 1997

James Lorimer & Company Ltd., Publishers
35 Britain Street
Toronto, Ontario
M5A 1R7

Printed and bound in Canada

Contents

For Cameron and Peter
— my big and bigger brothers.

1

Kate the Snake

Katie could see her whole world from up here. She looked at the ranch with its many outbuildings and the cattle spread across the pastures like black and white and brown ants. She could see a truck raising dust on the long tree-lined drive to Mr. Foster's farm. In the distance, her small town's church steeple gleamed white in the bright sunlight.

The path to Katie's secret place was steep, but her mare Fudge was, in Katie's view, about the most sure-footed horse in Alberta. In the short time that Fudge had been Katie's horse, they'd ridden up here many times.

Leaving the rolling pasture behind, they would ascend into the trees that covered the hillside. Gnarled roots snaked across the path where the spring rains washed the soil out from under them. At the first plateau, to the left of a huge boulder that jutted out into thin air, was a clearing, just big enough for a girl and her horse. A smooth hollow in the rock, where it joined the ground, provided Katie a cool, comfortable place to read and think.

Anyone seeing Katie aboard Fudge would think she was much younger than her actual age. She was small for thirteen, and with her short-cropped blond hair, she was sometimes mistaken for a boy. Katie looked barely able to handle a big horse like Fudge, but she had learned to ride almost before she could walk and her natural ability had been evident from the beginning.

On this warm, clear Saturday in mid-June, Katie was bursting with anticipation for the coming holidays. Very soon school would end. Although home chores would increase, there would still be plenty of time to ride. The crowning glory of the summer would be the Heritage Days Jamboree and Rodeo. For the first time, Katie had a shot at winning the junior girls' barrel race. Since March, when she'd inherited Fudge from her big brother John, Katie had been dreaming of the event.

Soon, Katie thought, I'll fill a wall with trophies just like Dad and John. Then everyone in town would agree that the Mavrinacs were the best show riders for miles around.

As if she could read Katie's mind, Fudge whinnied in agreement. Katie patted Fudge's neck. Swinging her leg over the horse's back, she slid to the ground. Taking a baggie of cut carrots and apples from her saddlebag, Katie shared her snack with the mare.

"I bet you're happy to have me aboard, instead of big, old John," she said. Fudge's big, soft mouth nuzzled her hand. "That's why we go like the wind, my girl. No big, stupid brother to weigh you down. Just little old me. And you wait, when we win the barrel race, we'll get a beautiful hand-tooled saddle in brown leather, just exactly the same colour as you."

Katie rested her head against Fudge's neck, while the big animal munched contentedly on the carrots. The saddle in question was the widely sought after first place prize for the girls' barrel race. Never before had there been such a prize in the Heritage Days Jamboree and Rodeo, not for the girls.

They had Felicity Fullerton to thank for the honour. Felicity had retired from the professional rodeo circuit two years ago and opened a tourist ranch where city people from the east came to ride horses and experience Alberta. Last year,

Felicity declared that the prizes awarded to the girls were sexist. She vowed that the following year she would donate something worth riding for. All of the young female riders in town waited with great expectation for the unveiling of the prizes at the town hall on the first day of June. Nobody had expected anything as beautiful as the tooled leather saddle that Felicity proudly revealed to gasps and enthusiastic applause.

Katie was so excited that she almost felt like crying. That was something that had been happening far too often lately. Her emotions were getting mixed up. When she was happy she felt like crying. When she was sad, sometimes she laughed uncontrollably at the stupidest things. Her mother said she vaguely remembered having similar feelings at Katie's age.

In the midst of her daydream, Katie heard the faint sound of an engine in the valley below. Paul was still quite far off, but Katie could clearly see her little brother. He was bouncing along in her direction, riding his favourite toy, an all-terrain vehicle.

Paul had never been to this spot, Katie had made sure of that. It wasn't his kind of place, anyway. Paul preferred wide open spaces where he could tear around, fast and furious on a horse, a bike or the ATV. Katie looked around her shadowy green and grey sanctuary and smiled. It was private, peaceful and hers alone.

But Paul knew the direction in which she usually headed, because he would sometimes accompany her as far as the ATV could safely go. Paul had a hand-me-down horse too, good, old, dependable Maude. Maude was not the swiftest of horses, but she was a good steady mare that had carried each of the three Mavrinac children. Maude had even posted some reasonable times in the barrel race in the last two years. But at eleven, Paul was at the age where driving a motorized vehicle was more exciting than riding a horse. Katie was happy to leave Paul to his motoring. The noise and the smell gave her headaches.

When Paul stopped the ATV and continued uphill on foot, Katie realized that he was probably looking for her. Rather than wait and risk being discovered in her secret place, Katie climbed back on Fudge and headed down the hillside to meet Paul.

"Looking for me?" Katie asked as she came upon Paul resting on a rock.

His face, surrounded by unruly, brown, curly hair, was reddened by the sun and wind. They had the same brown eyes, but there the resemblance ended. Paul was squarely built, like their father, with a big head. Ever since he'd been a baby, people had commented on his looks. Katie never remembered anyone fussing about her wispy, yellow, chicken hair like they did about Paul's soft curls.

"Yeah. Did you see me from up there?" he replied.

"I can see everything from up there," she answered, laughing. "Do you want to go riding?"

"Nah, Dad wants you. One of the calves is stuck between the barns."

"So?" Katie didn't see how she fit into the picture.

"The calf is kinda stuck in the middle and nobody else can get in there to push him out."

It was true. The space between the machinery barn and the feed barn was very narrow. Katie found it an ideal place to hide when her family got tiresome. Even though Paul was two years younger, he'd grown bigger than Katie by the time he was nine. For four years, Katie's little lane had been a narrow, but effective, refuge.

Brother and sister raced back to the ranch, but it was no contest. Katie and Fudge could handle the uneven ground far better than Paul on his all-terrain vehicle. See, Katie thought, as she rode up to the house, they can't improve on the horse.

A combination of lofty wooden and plain steel-sided barns ringed the family home. Two stories high, with an open veranda on two sides, the white wood-frame house had been Katie's father's childhood home. Apart from the wallpaper, little had changed inside since her father had been a boy. But outside, many barns and buildings had been added over the years to house the modern machinery and growing herd.

Outside the barns, Katie's dad, her handsome seventeen-year-old brother John, and Chuck, one of the ranch hands, were laughing and joking.

"Paul, take care of Fudge for your sister," their dad said.

Katie was amazed. It was rare that Katie played an important role in the working of the ranch. Everything was clearly organized around male and female roles. The men managed the stock and maintained the ranch and its property. The women cooked, kept the house and the garden and fed the chickens. It was pretty much the same at any of Katie's friends' farms.

"How did he get in there, anyway?" Katie inquired. "He must be awfully small."

She peered at the calf tightly wedged in the space. She suspected that any one of the others could squeeze in sideways, but they probably wouldn't like it.

"Go around the back, Katie, and give him a push. That might be all he needs."

Obediently, Katie marched around the barn and entered the narrow space behind the calf. In the dim light, it appeared that the calf might really be stuck and not merely frightened. Katie sniffed the air in the tight space.

"Somebody get me my rubber boots!" she shouted, backing out. "It's pretty messy behind that calf."

"I could have told you that!" laughed John.

Except for a few pounds and a mustache, John could easily be mistaken for his dad. The three Mavrinac men had dark, brown, curly hair. Katie's dad's was cropped quite short, John's a shade longer and Paul's longer still. They were like those Russian dolls that open to reveal smaller and smaller identical dolls inside. Katie, in her own view, looked like a mutt, with her dad's eyes, her mom's build and her grandmother's hair.

"Well, thanks for warning me," Katie retorted. Paul returned with the boots. Katie pulled them on, threw a defiant look at her smirking big brother and marched back into the space.

Speaking softly, Katie approached the calf. She believed in talking to animals. She'd been surrounded by them all her life and she'd found them to be great listeners. At least with animals you weren't disappointed when they didn't respond.

Gently, she reached out and touched the calf on the rump. He twitched his tail in reply. For a few moments, Katie just talked and petted the little animal.

"What's going on in there?" her dad called out.

"I'm trying not to spook him," Katie replied, keeping her voice low. "Just be quiet, okay?"

Ever so gently, Katie began to push the calf along. He didn't, and probably couldn't, budge. The calf had reached a place where the space narrowed just enough to offer resistance and there he was stuck. Katie leaned against the corrugated metal of one barn and slowly walked her feet up the side of the other one. Pushing with all her strength, she was able to flex the metal wall of the barn enough to give the calf some room. The sound echoed in the small space. Scrunched with her knees tight against her chest, she was barely able to slap the calf on the rump. After a few feeble swats, she finally managed to hit the calf and he grunted as he shot forward. The rest of the alley was wide enough for him to plow on through.

Katie emerged to cheers from her father and brothers.

"Smart thinking, Katie," her dad said, patting her on the back. He turned to John and Chuck. "Why didn't one of you guys think of that?"

Katie swelled with pride. She rarely received praise from her father.

"I'd have got stuck in there, just like that calf," John replied. He waved in the direction of Chuck, who was leading the calf back to the pasture. "There's barely enough room in there for a snake." He looked over at Katie, who was still flushed with pride and exertion. "Yessir, that was definitely a job for Kate the Snake."

Katie's bubble of pride burst as her dad slung his arms over the shoulders of his two sons. They laughed heartily as they walked away, leaving Kate the Snake behind.

2

Monday Morning Blues

No matter what time she went to bed, morning always came too early for Katie. A ranch is definitely the wrong place for someone who's not a morning person. Every morning, Katie would struggle out of bed and into her clothes. She would wander, half-asleep, into the chicken coop.

"Good morning, chicken little, chicken big, chicken fat. Oh sorry, I didn't mean to hurt your feelings," she said in greeting to the thirty hens. "Can I have this?" she inquired, reaching under a bird to extract a warm brown egg. A quick search of each roost yielded almost two dozen eggs. "Thanks, girls!" Katie said cheerfully, finally awake. "See you later."

Her first stop was the cookhouse where the ranch hands prepared their own breakfast. The three men took half of the eggs. The rest went into the house for the family. Nobody knew more ways to cook eggs than Katie's mom. That was okay with Katie, because she didn't like cereal and milk.

The heavy, cast-iron frying pan was all ready on the big old stove, with a puddle of bacon fat in the centre. Deftly, Katie's mom cracked the eggs, one-handed, and dropped them into the sizzling fat. The aroma of the bacon waiting in the warm oven filled the large room. John and Paul placed a stack of plates on the long pine table beside the three plastic glasses containing the cutlery. Taking their places, they waited expectantly for their breakfast while Katie made toast.

Once the food was on the table, Katie's mom spread lunch fixings on the butcher block counter. "Ham or baloney?" she asked, waving a butter knife over eight slices of thick, white bread.

"Baloney," Katie replied.

"Baloney," Paul chorused.

"Salami," interjected John.

"No salami. Ham or baloney," said his mom.

"Baloney *and* ham," John answered.

His mom slapped thick-cut slices of baloney and cured ham onto the bread with one hand, while swiping yellow mustard over the meat with the other. With assembly-line efficiency, she put the sandwich together, cutting it diagonally with a deft stroke of the knife.

As usual, Katie dawdled over breakfast, reading a paperback novel. The school bus horn wrenched her back to reality. Two more weeks of school. Yuck, Katie thought. She looked around and realized that her brothers were already gone.

Katie stumbled out the door, trying to stuff her book into her backpack. She hated being watched by the other kids on the bus as she raced up the lane. The bus driver, Mrs. Hapgood, would always say something about the Mavrinacs being the only kids on her route who weren't waiting at the corner when the bus came. As she ran, Katie prayed that she wouldn't trip and fall or do anything that would make the other kids laugh at her.

Fortunately, nothing horrible happened to her on the dash to the school bus. A breathless Katie took her usual seat beside Monica.

"You're always slowest on Mondays," Monica observed, her blue eyes sparkling behind her glasses.

"Oh yeah?" Katie retorted, "I'll race you around the schoolyard when we get to school."

"That's not what I mean," replied Monica. "You're later on Mondays than any other day of the week."

"So what?"

"Nothing. Just an observation," said Monica.

For a few moments, the girls sat in silence while the rest of the kids on the bus made a racket. Katie had the uncomfortable feeling that someone was watching her. Sure enough, when she turned around, Paul and his friends were staring at her with big grins on their faces.

"What?" Katie shouted above the noise, thoroughly annoyed. "What are you looking at?"

This made the eleven year olds grin and laugh even more. Paul was laughing the hardest. Katie jumped out of her seat. She made her way to the back of the bus where Paul and his friends were seated.

"Sit down, Katie Mavrinac," Mrs. Hapgood shouted sternly.

Katie looked around for somewhere to sit.

"Move over, Paul," she demanded. Paul scooted over a tiny bit, leaving hardly enough room for a baby to sit down. The kids started giggling, while Paul sat there with his big toothy grin.

"Katie Mavrinac," Mrs. Hapgood bellowed. "You sit down this instant or I'll stop the bus!"

Defeated, Katie stomped back to her seat beside Monica while Paul and his friends made strange hissing sounds.

"What was that all about?" Monica asked.

"How should I know?" Katie replied, exasperated. "They wouldn't let me sit down."

"They're just little kids," Monica said wisely from the distant perspective of her two additional years. "They live to annoy us. Ignore them."

The bus made its final stop before arriving at the school. They picked up Tracy, Katie's other best friend. For the rest of the ride, the three girls chatted about their weekends. Katie wished that her friends lived closer to her. The huge distances between their ranches made it difficult for them to get together on weekends. Katie hated to rely on her parents to drive her everywhere. They considered it too far for her to travel on horseback to either Monica or Tracy's house, although Katie didn't think so.

Paul's goofy friends were still making hissing noises and casting weird looks in Katie's direction, right up until the time they went into class.

The lower school and the high school were joined together by a long, covered corridor. Katie and her Grade 8 classmates were all looking forward to taking the walk down that corridor. It would signify their entrance into high school and near-adulthood. Once there, they would join the ranks of students who looked back with mild disdain at the public school with its small, scarred desks, low water fountains and supervised recesses. They longed for the exciting ways of high school, where they would move from class to class like mature students. But that was nearly three whole months away.

Later that morning, while Katie, Monica and Tracy enjoyed their lunch on a bench in the schoolyard, Paul and his friends gathered a short distance away, laughing and pointing at Katie.

"Hey, Kate the Snake," shouted Billy Larson. "Is it true you can slither under doors?"

Katie blushed red, feeling the heat rise to the tips of her ears.

"Shut up, Billy," she snapped.

Paul's bunch of rowdy friends circled the bench.

"What kind of snake are you?" snickered one of them.

"Garter snake," said Kevin MacDonald.

Katie jumped to her feet. She whirled angrily on Kevin, poised to fight. At eleven, Kevin was much heavier than Katie. Monica and Tracy leaped to her defense.

"Go away, lard butt," Monica shouted.

"At least I don't take up two seats on the bus," Katie added in her own defense.

Seeing Kevin blush, Katie immediately felt ashamed of herself for making fun of him just because he was overweight. The kids quickly disbursed as Miss Turnbull, the Vice-Principal, came over to investigate.

Sitting back down, Tracy soothed her friend's ruffled feathers.

"Good things come in small packages," she said.

Thoughtfully, Katie asked, "Why is it okay to make fun of small people, but it's not okay to poke fun at fat ones?"

"I don't know," said Monica. "Maybe because it's worse to be fat."

"Well, I'd rather be tall and fat than short and skinny. If I was tall and fat, I could lose weight any time. But I can't get taller just because I want to," Katie answered.

"Oh, you'll grow some more. You'll be tall just like your dad and your brother," said Tracy.

"Or short like my mother," replied Katie bitterly. "Can we talk about something else, please?"

Monica agreed. "You pick, Katie," she encouraged.

"Okay," said Katie. "Let's talk about the rodeo."

3

A Load of Trouble

John swung the pick-up truck with the double horse trailer attached in a wide arc, stopping abruptly in front of the horse barn. Katie coughed, half in earnest and half in protest, as a cloud of dust settled on her.

"Thanks, John," she said with sarcasm. It was lost on her brother.

"Sure, kid," he replied. "What are you waitin' for? Get your horse."

Shaking her head, Katie disappeared into the barn as John lowered the ramp. If it wasn't dust, it would be mud or gravel. Whenever John drove the truck, Katie thought, she was sure to be pelted with something.

Katie looked at the sky as a cloud passed over the sun. The temperature dropped instantly, warming moments later when the sun peeked through again. She would need a jacket for sure, she thought, knowing it would be cooler still in the deep woods.

It was the first trail ride of the season and all three Mavrinac kids would be showing off their new mounts. John on his new horse, Rob Roy, would be the envy of his friends. All the girls would make a fuss over him. Big deal, thought Katie, he's just a goof on a fast horse.

Paul, who should have been getting Maude out of her stall, was nowhere in sight. Katie sighed at the unreliability of brothers and went to get Maude herself.

"Come on, old girl," she soothed, leading the sway-backed sorrel mare out of the barn.

In her long life, Maude had been in and out of a trailer more times than anyone could count. She was the easiest one to load. They put her in first, as an example to other horses.

Katie gave Maude a treat before she went back for Fudge. Maude nuzzled Katie gently and for a moment Katie felt guilty about how easily she had transferred her affections to Fudge. Until a few months ago, Maude had been her horse.

"Don't worry, Maudie," she whispered. "I won't neglect you, even if Paul does."

"Get a move on, Katie!" John shouted. "Where's Paul?"

"How should I know?" Katie retorted. "Who made you boss anyway?"

"I just don't want to be late," John replied.

Katie went back into the barn, thinking that John wouldn't want to miss one second of all the attention he expected to get. Moments later, Paul rushed in.

"Where were you?" Katie asked. "I already loaded Maude."

"Yeah, thanks," Paul replied. "I was cleaning my boots."

Katie looked down at her little brother's feet. They were streaked with dust. "Why bother? They're already dirty again."

Paul looked sheepish. "I stepped in some … "

"Get the saddles, okay?" Katie interrupted, laughing. She slipped into the narrow stall beside Fudge and unclipped her bridle.

"Come on, beauty," she said, smiling. "Let's go win a ribbon."

Katie had another guilty moment as she admired her new horse. A full twenty centimetres taller and much prettier than Maude, Fudge was definitely a step up the equine ladder for Katie. Not only that, Fudge was a lot faster, although speed was only part of the skill needed on a trail ride. Katie's excellent sense of direction and her attention to detail had always helped her on the trail. Winning required a combination of horsemanship and problem-solving. Despite her lack of speed, Maude was a good trail horse, sure-footed and steady. It would be very interesting to see how well Katie would fare on Fudge. Of course, John had won many a trail ride aboard Fudge in the past, but he relied on speed to make up for wrong turns and missed checkpoints.

By the time Katie led Fudge out of the barn, John had positioned the old single trailer beside the tandem.

"You want a hand?" John asked.

"Okay, sure," Katie answered, although she was quite certain she could do it herself.

With Katie at her head and John behind, Fudge stepped onto the ramp. For a moment she hesitated, her head rising up. Katie pulled down hard on the lead, reaching out to stroke the horse's neck.

"It's okay, it's okay," she murmured, pulling gently forward.

For once, John let her take charge. Without further trouble, Fudge clattered up the ramp and into the stall beside Maude. Gleefully, Katie squirmed in beside her.

"Good girl!" she exclaimed. "Wasn't she a good girl, Maude?"

"Katie!" John yelled. "Hurry it up!"

Quickly Katie fed Fudge and Maude some carrots. She slipped back out of the trailer as John led Rob Roy out of the barn. The big chestnut stallion stood calmly enough as John dropped the ramp. Katie offered Rob a carrot which he took with enthusiasm.

"Hey, knock it off with the carrots," John protested. "You'll spoil him. He's a working horse, not a pet. I don't want him constantly looking for carrots and stuff."

"You're just too lazy, John, and you know it," Katie retorted. John wouldn't even know where to look for a carrot.

John took Rob by the bridle and led him to the ramp. About one metre from the edge, the horse stopped dead. John pulled insistently on the lead, while Rob pulled back just as insistently. With a shrug, John walked Rob around in a wide circle behind the trailer, leading him back to the ramp.

Again Rob stopped short.

"Okay, Katie," he said. "Give him a shove."

Cautiously, Katie slapped the horse's rump. Abruptly he stepped forward and just as quickly backed away.

"Let's try blindfolding him, Kate."

Handing Katie the lead, John took off his neckerchief and wrapped it around the horse's head, covering his eyes. It was clear Rob didn't like this any better than before.

John decided to switch places with Katie. To her dismay, he gave Rob a vicious whack on his rump. The horse reared up, pulling Katie off her feet. Still clinging to his lead, Rob dragged her across the yard at least fifteen metres before John caught up and stopped him.

Katie struggled to her feet, now completely covered in dust and dirt.

"You idiot," she shouted angrily. "What a dumb idea!"

She snatched the blindfold off the horse before John led him back toward the trailer.

"Sorry, Katie," John said sheepishly. "I'm going to get Dad to help. Hold him, okay?"

Without a word, Katie took the lead from her brother, who truly did look sorry.

"Stupid, stupid, stupid," she said to the horse, taking another carrot out of her jacket pocket. "I don't mean you Rob. Sorry, it's kind of dirty."

The horse took the carrot and munched on it quietly.

Katie looped the lead around the bumper of the single trailer, leaving the horse for a moment to retrieve her backpack. She rummaged inside, pulling out a large zipper-baggie bursting with carrots and apples. Returning to Rob, Katie unfastened his lead from the bumper and opened the baggie, careful not to spill its contents onto the ground. As Katie waved the bag under Rob's sensitive nose, the horse inched forward, questing after the enticing aromas. Smiling to herself, Katie backed carefully up the ramp.

"Come on, big fella," she crooned. "You can have two whole apples if you just follow me."

Rob stepped forward again. As soon as his front hoof clomped onto the ramp he stopped, hesitating between the alluring apples retreating with Katie into the trailer and the solid ground outside. Katie stepped forward, holding a quarter apple just in front of Rob's nose. The whole time, Katie whispered soothingly to the big horse. Finally, Rob gave in to temptation and clattered forward up the ramp. The noise of his hooves seemed to frighten him, but before he could change his mind, Katie snatched his bridle and stuffed the apple between his teeth. Moments later, Rob was secured in the trailer.

By the time John got back with his dad, the ramp was up and Katie was piling the saddles into the pickup.

"Hey, how'd you do that?" John queried.

Katie smiled smugly and said, "You can load more horses with apples than you can with blinders!"

"Good work, Katie," her father said, smiling. Turning to John he remarked, "Maybe we should store our apples in the trailers."

4

Trouble on the Trail

The field was already buzzing with people and horses when the Mavrinacs arrived. Anxious to be the centre of attention, John insisted on unloading his horse first. Katie helped by backing Rob out of the trailer. He seemed so happy to be free that Katie wondered if they would be able to trick him into getting back in it again for the ride home. Oh well, she thought, he'd better get used to it. There would be a lot of trailer rides in his future.

When all three horses were safely out of the trailers and saddled, Katie went off in search of Monica. Eventually, she spotted her standing impatiently by the registration table.

"You're late!" Monica said in greeting.

"I know, I know," Katie replied. "We had some trouble loading Rob Roy."

Monica scanned the crowd. "Where is John now?"

Katie looked at her friend with mild annoyance. Even Monica was dazzled by John. "Over there with his friends and Jenny Briscoe."

"Oh," said Monica. Thirteen-year-old Monica was no match for pretty Jenny Briscoe. Jenny was the star centre on the high school basketball team.

"He's a jerk," Katie said emphatically.

"Well, he's always been very nice to me," Monica replied in John's defense.

"You're not his sister. Let's sign up," Katie suggested, ending the discussion.

Katie and Monica collected their assignments, one of four possible routes around the course. Each rider had to pass thirteen checkpoints on their assigned route, in the correct order. The riders would be sent out in shifts, five minutes apart, four riders in each shift. With riders crisscrossing all over the trail, it could get pretty chaotic if you didn't read your route map carefully. Waypoints were a combination of clues, markers and tests of horsemanship. Each trail ride was a masterpiece of planning and organization on the part of the committee. They had spent countless hours cleverly devising the complicated routes.

At the start, each rider received cryptic instructions on how to find their first checkpoint. There they would receive the next instruction and so on until all thirteen checkpoints had been passed. The younger kids only had eight checkpoints to pass and they got lots of extra help.

"I'm rider thirty-three, route number four," Monica said, pulling her marker over her head. "What about you?"

"Rider thirty-four, route number two," Katie answered.

"We better get going. Our start's in ten minutes and I have to look this over."

Katie and Monica parted company, heading off to their waiting horses.

From the starting line, the path to Katie's first checkpoint was almost due south. She checked the compass hanging around her neck, although her keen sense of direction already told her where the path would likely be found.

"Are you ready, girl? I'll tell you what, you can have one carrot at every checkpoint and two if you get us there on time. Deal?"

The brown-eyed girl and the brown-eyed horse gazed intently at each other. Katie made a final check of her saddle, giving the cinch another tug for good measure. The bag of carrots was tucked into a saddle bag with her water bottle and some sandwiches.

Katie swung up into the saddle, lifted the reins and gave Fudge the signal to get moving. Fifty riders were competing and more than half had already left the start, including Paul. Spying Monica waiting in the on-deck area, Katie trotted over to join her and the other two riders who would be starting with them. As soon as the previous group left the start the four riders moved into position. Monica had the outside right position, with Katie second from the left.

The starter began the countdown from thirty seconds. The four riders watched the flag raised above his head. Five, four, three, two, one. The flag dropped and the four riders spurred their horses forward. They raced together between the two poles that formed a gate and separated. Each made a dash for the trees and the path that would lead to their first destination.

Katie had memorized the instructions: 170 degrees into the trees, keep to the right of the tree with the blight, red marks the turn to the left, snakes sleep here, on you go.

The trick was to keep the horse moving while scanning the area for landmarks. Katie knew that she could rely on Fudge to keep her footing, but a good rider kept an eye on the ground herself. The instruction sheet said that the target time for this leg was eight minutes. A quick glance at her watch showed Katie that they were three minutes into the event as they passed a tree split down the middle by lightning.

"This is our tree, Fudge," Katie said, laying the reins across the horse's neck. Immediately, Fudge veered to the right, jumping neatly over the charred branch that lay across the path. Bending low against Fudge's neck, Katie was able to clear the lowest branches without slowing the horse's pace. There were lots of branches that taller riders would have to duck, but Katie and Fudge sailed under. At least that was one advantage to being short.

Comfortable in the rhythm of the loping horse, Katie nearly missed the scrap of red fabric tacked to a sapling.

"Whoa, Fudge," she cried, reining the horse in.

Rather than stray from the path, Katie wisely chose the slower route of backing her horse up. Although the ground on either side of the path looked firm enough, the dead leaves might cover a groundhog hole or some other hazard. It was way too early in the game to take those kind of chances. Tugging gently on the reins, Katie eased the horse back the ten feet by which they'd overshot the turn.

"Git up," she encouraged, letting the horse have her head.

Katie was certain that the next turn was a large, flat rock in a clearing. It was like a big sun dial, the only spot where the sun penetrated the deep cover of the trees.

Through the trees she could see horses and riders criss-crossing ahead. The path dipped into a gully with a muddy bottom. Katie leaned back in the saddle as the horse eased down the slippery slope. Charging up the other side, Katie finally spied the first checkpoint. Fudge needed no urging as they sped up to the spot where Mrs. Forlow was parked in her lawnchair.

"What's my time, Mrs. Forlow?" Katie inquired, checking her watch.

"It's 143.09. Take this and get on your way." Mrs. Forlow marked Katie's time on her sheet.

Katie squinted at the next set of directions while rummaging in her saddle bag for Fudge's promised treat. Clamping the directions in her teeth, Katie leaned over to aim a carrot at Fudge's mouth, while taking a compass bearing to the next point.

"Eat fast, girl," she exclaimed. "I'm ready to roll."

The trail leading to the next point was arrow straight for an eighth of a kilometre, so Katie gave Fudge her head. They barrelled down the leafy lane, with the mare's hooves beating solidly on the packed earth. Joyfully, Katie allowed herself a big grin. This is the best, she thought, racing through the woods. She was oblivious to the fact that those woods were crawling with other kids, all bent on winning. To Katie, it was just she and Fudge, all alone, riding for glory.

A short distance ahead a log lay across the trail. Just beyond the log was a decrepit lean-to where they had to make a sharp turn onto a path that angled back. Katie dug her knees in, preparing for the jump. Horse and rider sailed over the obstacle with ease, but reining Fudge in quickly proved difficult and they overshot the turn. Carefully Katie steered her horse around the lean-to on the outside curve of the path. Twigs snapped under the horse's feet. An unseen creature stirred in the leaves.

Back on the right path, Katie was a little more careful. Since it led downhill, she had to rein Fudge in. It was darker in this area and she was grateful to see other riders ahead.

Intent on her mission to find the tree "wearing a coat," Katie didn't see another horse shoot up the embankment until it was too late for both of them. Fudge, frightened by the animal lunging out of the ravine, reared up, throwing Katie off balance. She felt herself slipping sideways off the horse. Grabbing for the pommel, Katie managed to hold on with one hand as her right leg swung free of the stirrup.

The other horse, equally spooked by the incident, bolted farther into the bush with its rider clinging for dear life. Her heart thumping, Katie dropped to the ground, anxious to quiet the frightened mare.

"I'm sorry, Fudge," she cried. "I know better. I promise I'll keep my eyes on the road, from now on."

Katie took a few deep breaths to calm herself. Looking around, she realized that there wasn't a trail where the horse had spooked them. Someone, Katie didn't get a good look at who it was, was either lost or taking an illegal shortcut. Whoever it was, they'd vanished.

Although she was anxious about lost time, Katie proceeded cautiously. She and Fudge soon found their next checkpoint, a tree with a yellow rain slicker hanging from a branch. Her sheet instructed her to walk her horse over to the coat. She had to put the coat on, take it off and return it to the tree. It sounded easier than it was. Her horse was not too fond of the spooky yellow form, and Fudge wouldn't stand still while Katie went through the motions. Somewhere, hidden in the brush, a trail judge was checking to see that Katie completed the task.

At the second-to-last checkpoint, and for the first time ever, Katie was two minutes ahead of the average time. She felt terrible for Darby Gaskell, who was bawling her eyes out on the trail. Not only had Darby lost her compass, but her directions were torn in two pieces. Since Darby wasn't in Katie's group, there wasn't much that Katie could do. She suggested in passing that Darby backtrack to the last checkpoint for another set of instructions, but this only brought on fresh tears and more anguish about the lost compass.

Seconds later, an entirely new animal crossed Katie's path. Her father, on the ATV, was bumping at full throttle along the trail.

"Dad!" Katie shouted, surprised to find him away from his post at the finish.

"Dad!" she yelled again, trying to make herself heard over the ATV's whiny motor. Her dad's head jerked up. Seeing Katie, he stopped the vehicle.

"John's in trouble," he exclaimed breathlessly. "Actually, it's Rob Roy. I've got to go. Tell your mother if you see her." With that, he sped off.

Katie hesitated, torn between finishing the race and concern for her brother and his horse. Her dad's expression had been so serious. But she was two minutes ahead! Her father was disappearing, with only the sound of the motor to mark his trail. Katie glanced back at Darby who was still crying beside the path.

"Darby! Come here!" Katie hollered. "Take this and get going."

She tossed her compass at the surprised girl. Without waiting for a reply, Katie spurred her horse in the direction that her father had taken.

5

Meanwhile Back at the Ranch

Katie urged Fudge along the trail, following her father as quickly as it was safe to do. Her dad was driving fast and the ATV bounced and shuddered ahead. Katie would often lose sight of him as he cut corners on the trail, but she followed the sound of the motor. She panicked for a moment when the sound cut out entirely. At the next turn, Katie was relieved to see the ATV stopped on the trail, with her dad and John just ahead, examining Rob Roy.

The big horse was bleeding profusely from a deep gash on his right flank at the top of the leg. Katie looked on with anguish as they attempted to slow the bleeding. Her dad turned around, looking anxiously back down the trail.

"Katie, go see what's keeping Doc Heslop," her dad said. "And then round up Paul and get the horses loaded. Your mother will drive you home."

Without hesitation, Katie wheeled her horse around and tore off along the trail. It wasn't until she was well out of sight of John and her dad that she reached into her jacket pocket for her map. She needed some reference to get her back to the start. To her dismay, after searching all her pockets and the saddlebag, the map was nowhere to be found.

A mixed sense of panic and frustration overcame Katie as she fought the urge to cry. If I go back, dad will yell at me, she thought. But what if I get lost? Oh, rats. Torn between riding off blindly or going back, Katie was rooted to the spot when Doc Heslop came charging up the trail.

"They're straight ahead, Doc," Katie said, pointing back along the trail.

"Thanks, Katie," responded the vet as he spurred his horse away.

"Wait!" Katie cried out, "I've lost my map. How do I get out of here?"

Doc Heslop reined in his horse, turned back to Katie and shouted, "There's a trail judge at the twin pines. She'll show you the way."

Relieved, Katie let Fudge carry her at a gallop to the spot where two large pines provided a canopy over the trail. Katie called out to the unseen judge who was monitoring a point nearby. A voice called back to her from the right, as Felicity Fullerton herself stepped out from behind one of the pines.

"Hello, Katie," she said, solemnly holding up a walkie-talkie. "I heard about John's trouble. Do you need some help?"

"I'm not sure where I am. How do I get out of here?"

Felicity pointed to her map.

"Here are the pines," she explained. "Take the left fork when the trail splits. Go slow and just follow the map."

Gratefully, Katie thanked Felicity who held up her walkie-talkie in reply.

"I'll let them know you're on your way out. It should take about ten minutes."

When Katie finally emerged from the forest, her mom and brother ran to meet her. Paul was chattering like a chipmunk.

"Did you see it? Was it bad? Was he bleeding a lot? John said it was really bad!"

"Shush, Paul," his mom said as Katie dismounted. She put her arm around Katie. "I'm sorry you didn't finish the ride, honey. From what I heard, you were well ahead on time and points."

Katie groaned. "I was winning?" she asked.

Her mom nodded.

"I'm not sure I needed to know that."

Much as she wished she'd been able to finish the trail ride, Katie knew that if her horse had been injured, she'd expect her brothers to rush to her aid. Actually, Katie thought, if it had been Fudge who was hurt, she'd want them to cancel the trail ride entirely.

As it turned out, it was Paul who had ridden to glory that day, winning his division by completing the course within a minute of the target time and by ten points on the horsemanship tests. Katie was further miffed by the fact that Maude had never once performed as well with her. But Katie could never be angry at any animal. She went about loading Maude and Fudge into the trailer as carefully as usual, while a little pot of resentment simmered away inside her.

Paul was unusually helpful loading the tack into the truck. Together, Katie and Paul made a thorough check of the trailer, the safety chains and the tires, just as they had been trained to do. Katie nodded solemnly to her mother, to indicate that they were ready to leave. With a last concerned look into the woods, Katie climbed into the truck. The three of them were mostly silent during the trip home.

What was left of the afternoon was spent in near mourning. Although Rob Roy's wound would heal, it posed a big problem for John. The horse would be out of commission for at least eight weeks, leaving John with no horse to ride in the Heritage Days Jamboree and Rodeo.

John's typical reaction to a problem was to sulk and lash out at anything, animal, vegetable or mineral. Katie, in a funk of her own, was inclined to stay away from John. Once her chores were out of the way at home, she was determined to slip away with Fudge to her secret place.

Although it was perfectly all right for Katie to ride off on her own, she wanted to make sure that no one discovered the route to her place. When it appeared that the rest of the household had gone about their business and that the coast was clear, Katie ventured to the horse barn to collect her saddle.

The tackroom was one of Katie's responsibilities. She was diligent about keeping the assorted equipment of horse riding and grooming in order. Curry combs and brushes hung on the peg board with bits and bridles. Reins and leads were coiled neatly. Saddles rested on sawhorses of various heights, with the stirrups hanging above the floor. It was an orderly room and Katie was justifiably proud.

When she entered the tackroom, Katie could see that something was amiss. John's saddle, which she herself had put in its place only two hours ago, was gone. A quick glance at the board revealed that a bit was missing. Perplexed, Katie spun around to face the stall where she was certain she had just seen Rob Roy. He was still there.

Katie ran outside to the paddock where Fudge and Maude grazed. One lone horse, Maude, stood lazily swatting flies with her tail. Annoyed, Katie scanned the horizon, spotting the distant profile of a horse and rider. John and Fudge slipped out of sight into a gully, as Katie kicked the ground in frustration.

Katie spent the rest of the afternoon in her room, a poor substitute for the calm of her secret place, and she was still angry when she came to the dinner table.

The events of the day cast a shadow over everyone. Even Paul was subdued, keeping his excitement in check. Katie felt very strongly that John should have asked her if he could take Fudge out, but the course of conversation at the dinner table didn't allow her the opportunity to raise the subject.

Ever since John had returned home from his ride, he'd been acting twitchy. It wasn't a much better mood than his previous one and for some reason it made Katie nervous. Sure enough, just as the family started dessert, John spoke up.

"You know, this is my last year in the junior rodeo," he began. "I sure would like to finish up with an unbroken record."

Something in John's voice made Katie suspicious, but when he resumed eating without further comment, she relaxed. She had just put a forkful of pie into her mouth when John cleared his throat.

"Anyway," John carried on. "I was thinking maybe I should take Fudge back for a while, you know, until after the rodeo."

Katie nearly choked on her pie. "What?"

John gave her a lame look.

"Come on, Katie," he whined. "You can have her back right after Heritage Days."

"What about me? What am I supposed to do?"

Katie gave her parents her most pleading look, fearful that yet again John would have his way.

"Well," her dad began slowly, "John has a point. He's got a title to defend."

"Get him another horse," Katie all but shouted. "Fudge is mine!"

"Everybody quiet down," her mom interjected. "This is an important issue. Let's discuss it calmly. Phil, Katie's right. Fudge is her horse now."

"That's right," Katie's dad said, addressing her now. "And Katie, if you don't want to let John have her, that's your decision."

For a moment, Katie felt the tide turn in her direction. Her father continued, turning now to John.

"I know how much this means to you, John, but unfortunately buying you another horse just isn't an option right now. You're welcome to take my horse, son."

"Oh, Dad," John groaned. "Ranger is no good for the rodeo anymore."

It was true. Katie's dad's horse was long past being competitive. John might as well take Maude as take Ranger. Once again, John turned his attention to Katie.

"I'd do it for you, Kate," John said.

Katie groaned. How many sacrifices should one person make in one day? She felt everyone's eyes on her. John's words echoed in her head, "I'd do it for you, Kate."

She was trapped. A voice she barely recognized as her own was speaking.

"Okay," she squeaked. If she hadn't been sitting down, she would have kicked herself.

6

Katie Evens the Score

I can't believe you gave him your horse," Monica said, shaking her head.

"What was I supposed to do?" Katie frowned. "I'd do it for you, Kate," she said in a mocking voice. "I bet you a million dollars he wouldn't. He'd find some good reason why he couldn't. And nobody would raise a finger to help me."

Self-pity washed over Katie as she sat morosely on the bench in the schoolyard with Monica and Tracy. They were waiting for the 4-H Club meeting to start.

"There must be a horse somewhere you can borrow," Tracy suggested.

"Yeah, sure. There are horses all over the county that their owners can't wait to get rid of," Katie replied bitterly.

Stung, Tracy got up to join another group of girls. Monica put her arm around Katie's shoulder and gave her a squeeze.

Her blue eyes were sympathetic as she said, "I know how much you want to win that saddle."

Katie looked up at her friend. Monica was every bit as competitive as Katie when it came to riding, but somehow she never let it interfere with their friendship. Katie wished she could be as generous as Monica. Of course, thought Katie, Monica is the oldest in her family. She's never had hand-me-down horses and ratty old hand-me-down saddles. Quickly, Katie banished those jealous thoughts from her mind.

"They're getting started," she said, rising to her feet. She looked at Monica, still sitting there with a concerned look on her face. "Thanks, Mon, you're the best." Monica smiled.

Mrs. Sampson, their club leader, had decided to hold the meeting outside because it was such a beautiful early summer day. In the late afternoon sun, kids of all ages were sprinkled around her on the school lawn. Today's meeting concerned the club's annual contribution to the Heritage Days Jamboree and Rodeo, the barbecue pit. Not one person visiting the event, resident or tourist, could leave without a taste of the finest barbecue in Alberta. Or so the club members would say.

They were here to work out the assignments, which rarely varied, but Mrs. Sampson prided herself on being democratic.

"We have some generous contributions to acknowledge, boys and girls," she began. "Thanks to the outstanding efforts of our hog-producing group, we won't have a repeat of last year's near-catastrophe when we almost ran out of ribs."

The beef-producing group applauded the hog-producers who accepted the recognition with a display of clowning and buffoonery.

"The generosity of the beef group is equal to or better than last year," Mrs. Sampson added. Again there was a round of applause, with the roles reversed. "Everyone is expected to contribute to condiments," she continued, when the applause died down. "I realize that it's too early for tomatoes, but I know there's plenty of relish and pickles to be had."

Katie was getting bored with the proceedings. This meeting had not varied as long as she could remember. Next they would drone on about the boys and the barbecue pit. Suddenly, Katie got an idea.

Not waiting for Mrs. Sampson's praise of Monica's mother's mustard pickles and Tracy's mother's corn relish, Katie raised her hand and waved it excitedly.

Mrs. Sampson stopped abruptly in mid-sentence. "Yes, Katie?" she inquired. "Do you have to go to the bathroom?"

The other kids tittered and giggled, while Mrs. Sampson looked expectantly at Katie.

"No, ma'am," she answered. "This year I'd like to work in the barbecue pit."

Mrs. Sampson looked puzzled. Heads snapped around in Katie's direction. Everyone held their breath.

"I'm sorry, Katie," said Mrs. Sampson. "I believe I didn't hear you correctly."

Katie repeated her statement and this time Mrs. Sampson's eyebrows disappeared under her bangs.

"But, Katie," she said. "The boys always do that."

Doggedly, Katie stood her ground. "Yes, Mrs. Sampson, I know they do. They did," she corrected herself. "But I want to do it too."

Katie's statement started a big hubbub among the kids. The meeting was perilously close to getting out of order.

"Well, we could take a vote," replied Mrs. Sampson.

Looking around, Katie realized that voting was not going to work to her advantage.

"A vote will just be the boys against the girls. There are more boys than girls here, so it wouldn't be fair," she pointed out. "If one of the boys wanted to serve condiments, would you make us vote on it?"

Mrs. Sampson was between a rock and a hard place. Katie was absolutely right. There was no point in a vote. But she wasn't going to let Katie off the hook that easily.

"If you work the pit, Katie," she said evenly, "someone will have to take your place in salads and condiments."

The kids began talking earnestly among themselves. Katie's unexpected demand had thrown the whole system into disarray, particularly since none of the boys would volunteer to step aside for Katie.

Once again, Katie defended herself.

"Mrs. Sampson, I don't see why I should do it *instead* of one of the boys. Why can't I do it *with* them?"

At this, Mrs. Sampson stood up to assert her authority. "Because, Katie," she said sternly, "there have always been just enough boys and just enough girls for the jobs. This would put the whole system out of balance."

Not to be denied, Katie fired her final shot. "All right, Mrs. Sampson. I volunteer my brother John to take my place."

Not being there to accept or not to accept the job, John was relegated to serving mustard pickles and corn relish. The thought gave Katie her first moment of pleasure in twenty-four hours.

When they arrived home, Paul couldn't wait to seek out John and tell him the news. Seconds later, John came storming out of the barn in a lather. Katie calmly explained to him how much it meant to her to be able to do this. As he began to argue, Katie cut him off neatly.

"I'd do the same for you, John."

Leaving him to kick and moan, Katie marched over to the paddock where the horses were.

"He better not take it out on you, Fudge," she said. "I never meant for it to happen like that, you know," she continued, talking to the horse earnestly. "I just wanted to do something different. They pushed me too far."

She leaned in to whisper, "I probably won't like it any better than tossing salads."

When her mom called her for dinner, Katie noticed that her dad's truck was gone. It was highly unusual for the Mavrinacs to start dinner without their father.

"Where's Dad?" Katie inquired when she entered the kitchen.

"He called and told us to start without him," her mother replied.

"Oh," Katie said, sitting down and still not knowing any more.

John sat in his seat, sending dark looks Katie's way. Their mom seemed pretty amused by the whole incident, and pretty soon the teasing started. John was quite hot under the collar. By the time their dad arrived, Mr. Mavrinac was brimming with excitement, not waiting to sit down before spilling his news.

"We've got a deal!" he exclaimed.

"That's wonderful, Phil," Katie's Mom said. "You'd better explain to the kids what's going on."

"Mr. Foster has sold us his stock," he said proudly. "And leased us the land to graze them."

Mr. Foster, who owned the next farm, had been struck by tragedy three times in short order. First, his arthritis worsened. Then, after a long illness, his wife died. Eight months ago his only child, Gary, was killed when he ran his truck off the road trying to avoid a stray cow. With no one to help him work the ranch, Mr. Foster had finally agreed to sell off the stock and lease his land to the Mavrinacs. Never a very pleasant man, Mr. Foster had become mean since Gary's death.

"It's a fair deal all around," Katie's dad continued. "I did have to make one small concession, though." He looked around the table at his audience. "I agreed to send Katie and Paul over to help him out around the house."

"Dad!" Katie and Paul groaned in unison.

"Oh, it's nothing. You'll just go over there for an hour or so, maybe one or two days a week. Paul can cut the lawn and mind the garden. Katie can clean the house and maybe do a bit of laundry. It's nothing."

Yuck, yuck, yuck, Katie thought. Two days a week at old Mr. Foster's.

"Just stay away from Midnight," their father warned.

Katie's ears pricked up. Her dad was talking about Gary's black gelding, Midnight Run — a horse just waiting for his owner to get rid of him.

7

Midnight at High Noon

"Come along, kids," Katie's mom called.

Katie wandered wearily into the kitchen where her mother was stuffing home-cooked food into a plastic bag.

"Katie, bring that casserole, please."

On the counter was a casserole dish, still warm from the oven. Katie picked it up carefully.

"Is he going to be there, Mom?" she asked.

"Oh, I think so, Katie," she answered. "He'll stay out of your way. You just vacuum around him if you have to."

Heaving a huge sigh, Katie dragged herself out to the car. Paul was playing fetch with the family dog. Hercules, a two-year-old German Shepherd, was named after Paul s favourite TV character. He was a big, friendly dog, clearly devoted to Paul. Seeing Katie and their mom coming out of the house, Paul hurried over.

"Can I take Herc, Mom?" he asked.

"As long as you keep him out of Mr. Foster's way," she answered.

Happily, Paul tossed the tennis ball into the back of the pick-up. Herc leaped after it and Paul hopped on behind him. Katie fastened the tailgate and joined her mother in the cab.

Normally, the kids would walk or ride their bikes over to Mr. Foster's place. This first time, their mom thought it would be neighbourly to bring something over with them. The ride took only a minute, all sixty seconds of which Katie wished that she was anywhere else on earth.

The Foster farm had a deserted look. The gardens had more weeds than flowers or vegetables. The porches had a thick layer of dust on them. The whole house, with its peeling white paint and crooked shutters, had a woeful look. A telling sign was the corral gate hanging open, as if to say that all the stock was gone.

It took Mr. Foster a long time to answer their knock. While they waited, their mom sent Paul to start pulling weeds in the vegetable patch.

The door finally opened and Mr. Foster stood looking at them, leaning on his cane.

"Hello, Vern," Katie's mother said. "I've brought Katie and Paul, and a few things for your larder."

Mr. Foster's answer was more grunt than greeting. But he stepped aside to allow them to pass into the kitchen.

"Vern, where are the garden tools?" Katie's mother asked.

Their mom had an easy way with everybody and Mr. Foster was no exception. She just treated him the same as she treated everyone else, not giving him any room to be grumpy.

After Katie's mom had put the food away and set Paul up with the garden tools and Katie with the cleaning supplies, she walked back to the truck.

"Keep smiling, kids!" she said, waving out of the window as she drove away.

With the curtains drawn, the house was dark and gloomy. Mr. Foster ignored Katie. He just sat in his recliner with the TV on and the sound turned off.

Katie laughed when she saw the vacuum cleaner. It was lime green and shaped like a ball. It didn't have wheels, which made it difficult to drag along. Katie plugged the vacuum into the only wall socket that was visible in the living room. It made a horrible racket when she turned it on. She gave the vacuum a hearty yank and yelped when the machine slid smoothly across the floor and banged into her shin. Carefully, she pushed the vacuum away and watched it glide across the wood floor. Weird, Katie thought, as the plug pulled out of the socket and the machine stopped moving.

"You never see a vacuum cleaner before, girl?" Mr. Foster said. "You gotta move the end with the hose around, too."

"I never saw one like this before," Katie replied. "It moves on air, or something."

"It's space age," said Mr. Foster, turning his attention back to the silent television.

Katie plugged the vacuum back in, so the noise would cover her laughter. More like ice age, she thought, as she vacuumed the living room floor, keeping a watchful eye on the fast-rolling canister.

Finishing downstairs, Katie began lugging the vacuum up the steps to the second floor. Mr. Foster banged his stick on the floor a couple of times to get her attention.

"Don't you be going into those rooms with the doors closed," he demanded.

"Yes, sir," Katie agreed.

Upstairs, four doors led off the central hall. Two of them, one on the right and one on the left, were open. Through the door on her right, Katie could see an old-fashioned, claw-footed bathtub with a mouldy shower curtain hanging on a ring suspended from the ceiling. The other room had a narrow bed, a dresser and a bedside table with a lamp. Except for the furniture and an ugly picture on the wall, the room was empty.

She wasn't sure what to do about the shower curtain, wondering how Mr. Foster could get into the tub by himself anyway. Katie decided to leave it. Giving the rest of the bathroom a decent scrubbing, she finished the upper floor quickly.

Grateful to be out of the house, Katie grabbed a broom and swept the porches. The clouds of dust she raised quickly settled right back where they had come from.

Paul was still pulling weeds, sweating in the sun. Hercules had found himself a shady spot for a nap.

"Paul," Katie called. "I'm going to have a look in that barn. Wanna come?"

Paul grunted in reply, flinging aside something green that looked suspiciously like lettuce. He followed his sister across the yard, glancing nervously back at the house. Katie stopped.

"Don't worry, he's watching TV," Katie said.

Inside, the barn was as dark as the house. Clean-swept, empty stalls stood open, except for one at the far end. Reverently, Katie and Paul approached. Through the bars, they could see a big, black horse standing quietly in the gloom.

Seeing Midnight, Katie remembered how magnificent Gary had looked, riding over to their ranch to visit them. She had had a big crush on Gary when she was younger. He was twenty-three when he died, not too much older than John. But his parents were much older than hers.

Lifting the latch, Katie slid the big door open.

"See if you can find a bridle, Paul," she whispered.

Paul scampered off.

"I wish I'd brought you something," she said to the horse, entering the stall slowly.

The big animal whinnied, pawing nervously.

"Don't you remember me, Midnight? Gary used to let me sit on you."

Paul came back with a bridle and a short lead. Katie took it from him, advancing slowly toward the horse. Midnight was dead still, staring calmly at Katie. She put out her hand to stroke his nose. He pulled back his head and the sudden movement caused Katie to jump. She paused a moment, letting the horse settle. Again, she advanced. This time the horse allowed her to touch him and put the bridle over his head.

It was as though a light went on in Midnight's mind. He bolted out of the door like he was shot from a cannon, pushing Paul aside on his way out of the stall. The barn door stood open and in a second he was out of it and sprinting around the corral.

Katie pulled Paul to his feet and the two of them raced out of the barn. Midnight was making a turn at the far end of the corral. In a flash, he was running back toward the two kids. Katie froze, hoping he would pass close enough for her to grab his bridle. Too late, she realized that the horse was headed straight for the open gate.

"Paul!" she screamed. "The gate! Get the gate!"

Caught between the horse and the open gate, Paul wisely chose to dive out of the way. Midnight was out of the gate in an instant.

All of his pent-up energy propelled the horse faster and faster, away from the barn and the house, into the wide open Alberta countryside.

Katie considered her options, which didn't include out-running a horse.

"Paul, run home and get Dad or John. Get Dad *and* John," she yelled. She was in trouble now.

Paul wasted no time, running across the fields in the direction of home. Meanwhile, Katie dashed off in the direction that the horse had taken, hoping to keep him in sight. Climbing onto the fence, she was peering into the distance when a gruff voice sounded from the house.

"You, girl!" Mr. Foster shouted. "What's going on here?"

Katie hesitated momentarily.

"Come over here, girl," he demanded gruffly.

Reluctantly, Katie climbed down from the fence, approaching Mr. Foster with dread.

"I'm not blind, ya know," he said. "I saw that horse. Ran right by the window, he did. How'd he get out of the barn?"

"I let him out, sir," Katie mumbled. "I meant to walk him in the corral, but he got away."

"You get that horse back in the barn if it takes you all night!"

With that, he turned awkwardly and stomped back into the house, slamming the door behind him.

Katie was thoroughly dejected by the time her father and John galloped up the lane. Pointing in the general direction of British Columbia, Katie watched them as they went in pursuit of Midnight. If she'd had a horse, she could have gotten him back by herself, she was quite certain. Of course, if she'd had a horse, she might not have been quite so keen to see Midnight.

8

Riding It Out

Katie was relieved when her dad and John came into view, leading Midnight. She ran to meet them.

"I'll walk him in, Dad," she said in greeting.

"I don't think so, Katie," her dad replied. "We don't want him running away again. Better let John do it."

"I can handle it, Dad," she replied.

Actually, Katie wasn't entirely sure she could, since Midnight had never given her the chance to lead him outside.

"But John can stay around, just in case."

Her father nodded. The two men dismounted, looping their reins over the top rail of the fence while Katie led the big horse into the barn.

John followed behind, securing the corral gate, while their dad went over to the house to see Mr. Foster.

"He's a beauty, eh John?" Katie marveled.

"If you like black horses," John replied. "It's a shame to keep him cooped up in here, though. You know Charlie Wilder, Gary's best friend? Dad says he feeds him and rides him when he can."

"I could do that!" Katie said, an idea forming.

"Dad says Mr. Foster's really weird about this horse. You'd better forget it."

They tossed Midnight some hay. Katie reluctantly slid the stall door closed. Outside, Ranger and Fudge stood quietly.

Katie's dad was standing on the porch of the house, talking to Mr. Foster through the screen door.

"John, can I ride Fudge home?" Katie asked, looking longingly at the horse.

"What am I supposed to do?" John replied.

"Walk. It's only a kilometre," Katie retorted. "That's how I was going to get home."

John, who wasn't used to walking any farther than he had to, was reluctant.

"Come on, John," Katie begged. "She's still my horse."

"Okay," John said grudgingly. "You can brush her when you get home."

Katie quickly drew up the stirrups to the first notch.

"Don't forget to put those back. And you can soap my saddle, too," John added.

"Don't push it," she said dryly.

Katie's heart was light as she sped away in a cloud of dust. From the Foster farm, the route up the hillside to her secret place ran parallel to the stream for two kilometres above the ford. The sun sparkled on the swift-moving water as it splashed and tumbled over the smooth rocks. Katie didn't have a watch, but judging by the position of the sun in the sky, she guessed it was close to four o'clock.

Although there would be plenty of daylight left, she had to be mindful of the time before dinner. As Fudge trudged up the hill, Katie let her mind wander over the events of the day.

"You know what, old girl?" she said aloud. "I'm going to ask Dad if we can borrow Midnight until the rodeo. That way he'll get lots of exercise and I'll get a horse to ride."

They arrived on the bluff overlooking the farm, and Katie dismounted.

From that height, the Foster farm didn't look run down. Fences stitched the landscape into a patchwork dotted with slow moving cows. Fudge butted her head into Katie gently.

"I'm sorry, Fudge. You're the second horse today that I haven't had treats for. I'll bring you something after dinner."

Tying her horse to a tree, Katie sat down on the grass. She turned her plan over in her head, thinking of the perfect way to make her request. She was fairly confident that she could make a convincing argument to her dad, but how he approached Mr. Foster was beyond her control. Her parents were very friendly toward Mr. Foster, although it was beyond Katie's understanding how anyone could be friends with someone that crotchety. She remembered Mrs. Foster quite well. She had been a warm-hearted, generous woman. Even before Mrs. Foster died, Mr. Foster was gruff and unpleasant. Now with both his wife and Gary gone, he was ... Katie stopped that train of thought. It would only shake her resolve if she thought about how mean Mr. Foster could be.

Suddenly, Katie jumped up. She quickly untied the horse and swung aboard. She urged Fudge downhill, anxious to get home, but it had nothing to do with being on time for dinner.

Fudge's hooves beat on the ground, in time with Katie's heart beating in her chest. Now that she had a plan, she was anxious to put it into action. She pressed Fudge forward and they sailed together over the shallow irrigation ditch that bisected the fields.

She rode the horse right up to the corral gate and walked her inside. Quickly, she removed John's saddle, leaving the bit and bridle on the horse. A light lather glistened on the horse's neck. She lugged the saddle into the tack room.

Without pausing to restore John's stirrups to their usual length, she grabbed her own saddle. John was standing in the tack room doorway.

"Hey, you said you'd adjust that," he said pointing to his saddle.

"I'm not done yet. Don't worry. I'll get to it." Katie pushed past him.

Outside in the corral, Katie hefted her saddle onto the fence rail. She fetched some water for the horse and then disappeared around the side of the barn. Three empty oil drums stood against the wall. Knocking the first one onto its side, Katie rolled it into the corral and positioned it in front of the barn door. She rolled the other two barrels into place on opposite sides, to form a triangle.

John watched her, but made no move to help.

"I rode her hard today, Katie. She's too tired for this," he said.

"Just twice around. That's all I want," Katie replied, defiantly.

It was worth it, for those few seconds of pure, concentrated riding. With Fudge saddled again, Katie walked her out of the gate at the end of the corral, into the near paddock. Taking the reins in one hand, she turned the horse to face the barn and the barrels.

"Git up!" she shouted, switching the loose ends of the reins over the horse's flanks.

Fudge bolted forward and Katie guided her clockwise around the barrel on the right. Her hooves churned the soil as she strained in the tight turn. Coming out of it, she bumped the barrel and it fell over.

As Katie concentrated hard on the counter-clockwise turn on the other side, John shouted, "Penalty!"

This time, Fudge made the turn cleanly. They raced to the end, taking the barrel on the right. They ran like the wind down the length of the corral and out into the paddock.

John righted the barrel as Katie shouted breathlessly, "I'm not timing this!"

Once John had gotten out of the way, Katie spurred the horse forward again.

Once again, the first barrel fell as they finished the turn. This time, the second barrel went down too. Switching the straining horse with the reins, Katie leaned low over Fudge's neck as they made the final dash.

Katie, exhilarated, flung herself out of the saddle and threw her arms around Fudge's neck. She wasted no time unsaddling the horse and slipping the bit from her mouth.

"Don't go away, I'll be right back," Katie said. Fudge wandered a short distance away to nibble the grass on the other side of the fence.

When Katie returned to groom her horse, John was rolling the barrels into place. "Don't forget my saddle!" he called to her.

"I know, I know!" Katie said. "I'll do it after dinner."

Throughout the evening meal, Katie was still elated about her ride, and somewhat jittery about revealing her plan to borrow Midnight. While she was still working up to it, her dad started talking about his conversation with Mr. Foster.

"He's very annoyed with you, Katie," Mr. Mavrinac said. "I told him you're normally quite responsible. Didn't I warn you to stay away from Midnight?"

"But, Dad," Katie defended herself. "I was just going to let him into the corral to stretch his legs."

Paul nodded in agreement, his mouth full of mashed potatoes.

"You leave that to Charlie Wilder. He takes care of that horse."

"Actually, Dad, I was thinking maybe I could do it for a while. Until the Heritage Days Jamboree. Then maybe I could ride Midnight in the rodeo. It would be good for him." Katie's mouth was dry at the end of her speech.

Her dad didn't even look at her. He just kept shoveling more food onto his plate.

"No. Mr. Foster is very peculiar about Midnight. He's not for sale."

"I don't mean we should buy him, Dad!" Katie's voice rose in pitch. "I just want to ride him for a few weeks, that's all."

Her mother interjected. "Katie, we know how hard it is for you, not having a horse to ride this year. But the situation with Mr. Foster and Gary's horse is very complicated. I think it pains him to let go, almost as if he'd be losing more of Gary."

"But, Mom." Katie could see her carefully reasoned argument collapsing. "We could bring him over here, Midnight I mean. Mr. Foster wouldn't have to see him."

"Forget about it, Katie," her dad said. "I won't waste my time asking him."

I'll just have to do it myself, thought Katie.

9

Walking on Eggshells

The following morning after church, Katie decided to hike up into the foothills with a book and her binoculars. Although she could read for hours on end, Katie liked to take a break now and then, to see how life was unfolding in the valley below.

She was in her bedroom organizing her reading material when her mother called from the kitchen. Katie shoved the last of her books into her red backpack and went to answer her mother's call. She slipped quietly into the kitchen.

Her mom was up to her elbows in flour and didn't hear Katie come in. She turned to reach for the butter on the table and gave a shriek.

"Oh my gosh, Katie," she laughed. "You scared me half to death."

"Sorry, Mom," Katie replied. "You called."

"Oh, yes I did. I promised to take some eggs to Mr. Foster today. Would you mind grabbing a dozen and taking them over? I'm up to my… you know."

In fact, Katie did mind. She minded a lot. Mr. Foster's house was the last house in Alberta she wanted to go to today.

Instead she said, "Okay. No problem."

Rummaging behind the pantry door, Katie extracted a cardboard egg carton.

In the yard, Paul was annoying Hercules with a stick. The big dog was trying to sleep, snuffling and twitching in the midst of a dog dream.

"Hey, Peewee, how about a trip to Frightenstein's house?" she called to Paul.

"Huh?"

"Mr. Foster's. I gotta take some eggs over. Wanna come?"

"Nah. I'm going to the auction," Paul replied.

"What auction?" Katie said suspiciously. Nobody had said anything about an auction today. At least not to her.

"At Fahrenbach's. Dad says they have a good tractor for sale. Me and John are going with him."

"John and I," Katie automatically corrected him while wondering why she hadn't been invited. "When are you leaving? Maybe I'll go too."

"It's men only," Paul said proudly, puffing up his chest. "Dad said."

"That's baloney!" retorted Katie, angered at the thought of the men in her family excluding her.

Stung, Katie strode to the henhouse, banging the door open and unsettling the hens.

Instead of her usual friendly greeting she barked, "Get over it!" at the birds.

Roughly yanking an egg from under a hen, she pitched it into the carton, but missed by a mile and the egg cracked on the floor. Katie ground it into the dirt with her boot, pulverizing the shell. She wiped her feet then took another egg. With each successive egg, Katie's anger mounted. She muttered unhappily about her unfortunate lot as a girl in a man's world.

Taking another egg, she purposely threw it against the henhouse wall, watching as the yolk ran streaming down the dark wood. As if possessed by demons, she flung several more eggs until the small building was splotched with yellow.

The hens clucked nervously, unused to the string of angry words that streamed from Katie. Finally, she grabbed the surviving dozen eggs and made for the door.

Surveying the mess she'd made, she remarked to the hens, "See, life's not kind to girls!"

Emerging from the henhouse, Katie saw her mother pop her head out of the kitchen window.

"Katie, I need two more eggs!" she called.

Knowing full well that there wasn't a whole egg left in the henhouse, Katie took Mr. Foster's dozen back into the henhouse with her. Extracting two eggs, she slipped them into her jacket pockets. Facing the mess for a second time, Katie sighed mightily and reached for the hose. When she finished hosing off the wall, she went back to her mother with the two eggs, noticing that the truck was gone.

On her mountain bike, Katie wheeled slowly in the direction of Mr. Foster's house, not for the safety of the eggs, but because she really didn't want to be going there.

She was relieved to discover that Mr. Foster wasn't home. Leaving the eggs on the back porch swing, Katie strode boldly to the barn. In her pack she had a baggie full of goodies for her hike, including some carrots and apples. At least she could make up for yesterday.

Being careful to close the corral gate and barn door behind her, Katie approached the stall, calling out to Midnight. Opening the stall door only enough to slip through, Katie greeted the horse heartily. She fed him everything in the baggie, which she thought he took gratefully.

"I bet you'd like a good combing," she said to him. Midnight neighed loudly as if in agreement. Katie slipped back out of the stall to search for the tackroom. Horse barns are all pretty much the same, and she found the small tackroom at the end of the row of stalls. She looked in awe at the walls, covered completely with blue ribbons, trophies and yellowing newspaper articles. It was like a shrine to Gary. Dust and cobwebs covered everything but the saddle. Katie guessed that Charlie had been around recently. Like John, Gary had been junior champion many times. Katie shivered involuntarily, as though Gary's spirit was still in the room. Quickly she grabbed a curry comb and ran back to Midnight's stall.

Once the big animal was brushed and shining, Katie lay back in the clean straw. She felt weighed down by the unfairness of her situation.

"We're sort of in the same boat," she said to the horse. "Something bad happened to somebody else, and we're the ones who suffer. It's not fair. It's not fair that Mr. Foster keeps you locked up because he can't stand the sight of you. It's not fair that I lost my horse because my dumb brother did something stupid."

Midnight's tail swished back and forth in agreement.

Katie continued. "I don't see why they won't let me ride you in the rodeo."

"I'll tell you the same thing I told your father, missy," barked Mr. Foster.

Katie jumped straight into the air. "I, I … I didn't hear you come back … " she stammered, wondering how much he had overheard.

The old man tapped his cane impatiently, as though waiting for Katie to come out of the stall.

"I'm sick of being bothered about that horse. You get out of there."

Edging through the opening, Katie retreated out of reach of Mr. Foster's cane.

"Get back here and shut that stall!" he shouted after her.

Still uncertain whether he meant to hit her, Katie approached cautiously. Mr. Foster stood still, scowling at her all the while. With the stall door closed and latched, Katie relaxed slightly. She wasn't sure if she should walk out of the barn ahead of or behind Mr. Foster, so they both stood quite still for a few awkward moments. Finally, Mr. Foster turned and walked slowly out of the barn. Katie followed, closing the door behind her.

"Um, sir," Katie stammered. "I brought some eggs for you. They're on the back porch."

"Thank your mother," he replied gruffly.

Katie felt a spark of anger at his ungracious reply. He could have thanked her too, for riding over and bringing them to him. Her anger made her bold.

"Sir? I meant what I said back there. It would be good for Midnight to be ridden regularly and I'd take really good care of him. It's just until the Heritage Days Jamboree. I'd really appreciate it."

Mr. Foster was awkwardly mounting the steps to the back porch. He turned sharply, sending his cane clattering down the steps. Katie ran to pick it up. He snatched the cane from her, his eyes blazing. "Not another word, young lady. Not another word about that horse!"

The screen door slammed behind him, punctuating his words.

10

The Pits

Summer was finally here. Just when June looked like it was going to last forever, school was out and the whole town was focused on the Heritage Days Jamboree and Rodeo, starting in just four weeks.

For Katie, however, summer holidays were going to be a mixed blessing until Rob Roy was well enough to ride and she could get Fudge back. It was hard to watch John tearing up the corral, practicing for his events.

Fortunately, that particular thorn in Katie's side would be absent for two whole weeks. John was leaving for his annual visit to their cousins' ranch near Innisfail. It was a good news, bad news situation, though. He would be taking Fudge with him.

It took all of Katie's self-control not to cry when her father called for her to help load the horse into the trailer. They were all outside, her dad, John, Paul and even her mom. Katie's Mom was loading hampers of food into the truck, while Paul struggled along with John's tack, the reins and stirrups dragging in the dirt.

John led Fudge out of the barn. At the sight of her, Katie felt her throat tighten. Tears of sadness welled up in her eyes. Hastily, she brushed them away, going forward to help John with Fudge.

"I'll walk her up," Katie offered, knowing that John would not be particularly gentle if Fudge balked.

"Go ahead," John said. "She's your horse."

Katie looked at John closely, to see if he was being sarcastic, but his bland expression didn't seem to hold any malice.

"That's right," she whispered to Fudge, leading her away from John. "You're my horse and don't you forget me while you're gone." Katie lowered her voice even more. "Just keep thinking about how nice it's going to be to have little Katie back in the saddle, instead of big, heavy John."

Reaching into her pocket, Katie produced a long, juicy carrot, with the top still on. She tickled Fudge's nose with it, all the while leading the horse up the ramp. Fudge went without a hitch and once there, contentedly munched on the carrot. John brought some oats out in a bucket, which Katie poured out into the feed trough.

Her dad came around the back of the trailer. "All set in there?" he inquired.

"All set, Dad," Katie replied with a sigh.

"Are you sure you don't want to come with us for the day, Katie?" he asked, as she scrambled out of the trailer.

Katie was quite certain she didn't want to make the trip with the rest of family. She liked her cousins well enough, but they were all boys and older than her. They used to play together when they were younger, but now they made it clear that Katie wasn't welcome in their activities. That left Paul, whom she could hang around with any day of the week.

Instead of going over to Innisfail with the family, Katie had arranged to spend the day with Monica.

"No thanks, Dad," Katie finally replied. "Stewey's loaning me his horse for the day."

Stewey was Monica's younger brother. Katie imagined that Monica had done a bit of arm-twisting to convince him to give up his horse on the first day after school let out. Katie had a pile of comics in her backpack for Stewey, to thank him for his sacrifice.

Sitting in the back seat between her brothers, Katie tuned out their loud voices. She had mixed feelings about seeing her brother off for two weeks. On the one hand, with John away, she would not have to watch him practicing with her horse. On the other hand, she would miss Fudge terribly. She was jolted out of her reverie as the truck turned off the asphalt highway onto the rutted drive to Monica's house.

Monica was waiting for Katie as the Mavrinac's pick-up with the trailer attached circled around in the yard. Katie's mom got out with her, disappearing into Monica's house for a few minutes to deliver a pie. Katie always thought it was silly that all the women around town exchanged food and baked goods. Monica's mother was a perfectly good cook, and Katie laughed when her mom emerged from the house carrying a different pie.

"My Mom says your Mom's peach pie is the best in the county," Monica said.

"She soaks the peaches in wine," Katie revealed.

"Wow," Monica marveled, "I'm going to have two pieces tonight!"

"You'd better not tell your Mom," Katie said. "I think it's a secret."

"Come on," Monica urged. "I've got the horses saddled and ready to go."

The two friends ran toward the barn, where Monica's and Stewey's horses stood ready. Katie adjusted the stirrups and checked the cinch.

"All set!" she announced.

The land around Monica's ranch was flatter than at Katie's. To Katie, it was monotonous, with little shade and only the river to make it interesting. But the flatter access roads provided excellent opportunities to let the horses run.

Although it was still early in the day, the sun was hot in the cloudless sky. The girls' route would take them past a dammed-up part of the river where they could swim. This early in the summer the water would be quite cold, but refreshing for a quick dip.

Monica led the way at a canter through the pastures where the cattle grazed. One of the family's dogs followed along a short distance behind. Periodically, the dog would dash off to herd some cows.

Stewey's horse, G-force, was a black and white pinto. At one time, the horse's name had been Foxfire, but Stewey had insisted on renaming him. Both Monica and Katie thought that Foxfire was a better name, so for today Katie called him that.

They cut diagonally across the wide pasture, heading for the river. In the far corner was a gate that opened onto an access road. Katie spurred Foxfire and they sped ahead of Monica.

"Race you!" Katie shouted over her shoulder.

She dug her knees into the horse, bending low over his neck. His hooves made a dull thudding sound on the lush grass. Air whooshed past her ears and she had to strain to hear Monica behind her.

She stole a look back and saw Monica was closing fast.

"Come on, Foxy," she urged.

Her heart began pounding, as though it was Katie doing the running. The gate was coming up fast. Rather than slow the horse and risk letting Monica overtake her, Katie steered the horse straight at it. Sneaking a quick look behind her, she determined that Monica was a nose behind and to her right.

The horse began to slow his stride, so Katie laid the reins over his neck on the right side. Foxfire turned in a smooth arc to the left just before the gate, running out of steam twenty metres along the fence.

"I win!" shouted Katie jubilantly.

By now Monica had the gate open and was steering her horse through.

"Don't forget to close the gate behind you!" she called out to Katie.

Monica sped away at full speed down the dirt road, leaving Katie in her dust.

Katie laughed good-naturedly, and led Foxfire through the opening. She closed the gate carefully behind her. By the time she was done, Monica had all but disappeared down the road. Instead of pursuing Monica at top speed, Katie let Foxfire lope along while she enjoyed the moment. In her mind, she imagined she was rescuing Midnight Run from Mr. Foster and they were on their way to a secret hideout deep in the forest. No one would find them there.

Katie imagined that Monica would bring food for her and Midnight. For four weeks Katie would train with Midnight, emerging from her hiding place in time for the Heritage Days Jamboree and Rodeo. Triumphantly, they would ride into the ring, to the amazement of the town. With astonishing speed and agility, Katie and Midnight would race around the barrels in record time. Newspapers all over Alberta would report her amazing feat.

Totally engrossed in her fantasy, Katie missed the track that led away from the road and down to the river. By the time she was imagining herself on national television, she was well past it. A thin voice calling her name drifted to her on the breeze.

Katie awoke from her reverie with a start. Concentrating on the sound of Monica's voice, she determined that the sound was coming from behind her. She turned Foxfire around and thundered back down the road. At the crest of a rise, she could see Monica waiting on the road ahead.

"Where were you going?" Monica asked, puzzled.

"Sorry, Mon," Katie replied. "I was lost in my thoughts."

"You keep going that way and you'll be lost in more than that," Monica laughed. "Come on, I'm ready for a swim."

Monica turned her horse down the path. This time Katie kept Monica within sight, and soon they arrived at the swimming hole.

Monica's dad had created the swimming hole by scooping out the river bed to form a deep pool. Dams at either end controlled the flow of water through the pond. Later in the summer, when the water had warmed up, it would be a popular place with their school friends. The only thing missing was a tree. It would have been fun to swing out over the water like they did in movies.

Unlike Monica who dove in straightaway, Katie preferred to immerse herself slowly. The water was bitingly cold.

Monica burst to the surface.

"Stop torturing yourself!" she called out. "Dive, Katie, dive!"

Ignoring her, Katie continued her slow descent. By the time she was completely wet, Monica was already out of the water, complaining of the cold.

Katie's departure from the pool was much hastier than her entry.

"Yeow!" she exclaimed, accepting a towel from Monica. "Why do we do that?"

"It's fun!" Monica towelled her long hair vigorously.

She whipped the towel off of her head, leaving her hair sticking out like a big brown nest. Katie laughed at the sight, dragging her towel over her own head. Her short blond hair was probably standing up on end just like her friend's.

With the sun warming them, the girls spread their towels on the ground. Monica pulled the picnic lunch her mother had prepared for them from her saddle bags.

"Wouldn't it be great to do this every day?" Monica asked.

"I'm not sure Stewey would be willing to give up his horse every day. I wouldn't," Katie said.

"Did you ask Mr. Foster about Midnight?" Monica inquired.

Katie groaned.

"I guess that means no," Monica said.

"Actually," Katie answered, "I did ask him. He just yelled at me. He said to stop bugging him."

"He's so mean," Monica said in sympathy. "He wasn't very nice before Mrs. Foster and Gary died. Now he's just awful. My aunt Clarice used to drive him to church, but now he refuses to go. He said praying won't bring them back."

"They probably wouldn't want to come back, even if they could," Katie said spitefully. Monica laughed.

"I'm going to ride that horse," Katie announced, tossing the pickles from her sandwich into the water. "If it's the last thing I do, I'm going to ride Midnight Run. Just you wait!"

"What are you going to do? Lock Mr. Foster in the house?" Monica asked. "Maybe you could put something in his tea to make him sleep."

"Don't make fun of me," Katie said hotly.

"I'm not making fun of you, Katie." Monica soothed. "I just don't think Mr. Foster is going to let you ride his horse."

With a furrowed brow, Katie took a big bite of her sandwich. "I know how to make him," she said. "You're going to hold him down and I'll feed him your mother's pickles until he begs me to take the horse away."

11

Midnight by Moonlight

Her brash statement to Monica may have been made in a moment of frustration, but when Katie thought about it later, the idea appealed to her greatly. Midnight Run had become a symbol of how her happiness was tantalizingly close, but obstinately out of reach.

During the lazy summer day that following her ride with Monica, Katie found herself thinking often of how exciting it would be to ride Midnight in the rodeo. Little pangs of conscience nagged at her, as her loyalty to Fudge wavered.

A day later, on her next duty visit to Mr. Foster's, Katie was thrilled when the old man began snoring loudly in his chair. She purposely ran the vacuum close to him. When he didn't wake, she scooted outside for a surreptitious visit to the forbidden horse.

"Hi, big fella," she crooned. "Did you miss me?" Katie pulled a shriveled apple from behind her back. "Sorry it's not too fresh. Just like Mr. Foster to let things rot!"

The horse took the apple she offered, as she stroked his gleaming black neck.

"I can't stay long, Midnight, but one of these days I promise I'm coming back and we'll go for a long, fast ride!"

Hastily, Katie shut the stall door and slipped out of the barn. She took the long way around, pausing to talk to Paul in the vegetable garden.

"Take some of those carrots out to Midnight," she instructed. "But don't let Mr. Foster see you."

Paul nodded absently, as he cultivated the rows. Reluctantly, Katie went back into the house where Mr. Foster's snores still rattled the china knick-knacks.

Katie wondered how long she and Paul would have to do this. If Mr. Foster's arthritis got much worse, he wouldn't be able to climb the stairs. Maybe, Katie thought, he'd move into one of those homes for seniors. A sudden image flitted through her mind: a middle-aged Katie feeding carrots to Midnight, his muzzle gray with age, while a wizened Mr. Foster, looking like one of those apple dolls, dozed in a chair covered with cobwebs.

The thought made her laugh out loud. Mr. Foster woke with a grunt.

"What are you laughing at, girl?" he demanded, gruff as always.

Stifling her laughter, Katie replied seriously, "Nothing much, sir. I was just thinking of a joke someone told me."

"Let's hear it, then! Let's hear what you youngsters find funny nowadays," he said.

Katie was shocked into silence. "Oh, it's not really funny. At least, not to you," she stammered, backing out of the room.

"I got a sense of humour, you know," Mr. Foster said. He turned in his chair, looking for Katie. She was long gone.

Outside, Katie spied Paul sauntering back from the barn.

"Let's get out here," she called. "You won't believe this, Paul. Mr. Foster asked me tell him a joke!"

"Get out of town," Paul snorted. "His face would crack in a million pieces, he'd, he'd … " Paul couldn't finish, he was laughing so hard himself.

Later that night, with the house all quiet and dark, Katie sat at her window looking out at the moon. It was late, after eleven. Usually she would be asleep by now, but her mind was unsettled, making sleep difficult.

"Probably moon madness," she said out loud.

As if in agreement, a coyote howled in the distance. The moon was so bright, it cast shadows. The long, thin shadow of the flag pole in their front yard was pointing right at Midnight's barn.

Katie got an idea. Stealthily, she dressed and crept down the stairs, avoiding the creakiest ones. At the bottom, she held her breath. There was nothing more than the usual creaks and groans of the house and the soft whir of an electric fan. She snatched up her boots and her backpack. Instead of leaving by the back door, she picked up the flashlight that stood on the shelf just inside the cellar. Shielding the beam with her hand, Katie used it to light her way down the cellar steps. From the coldroom, she took a bunch of carrots and a few crisp apples, stuffing everything into her pack.

Katie unlocked the door that led outside from the cellar. The light of the moon was bright enough to see by, so Katie stowed the flashlight in her pack. She hesitated, deciding whether to walk or to take her bike. With the bike she would have to stick to the road, which would make it difficult to hide if any vehicles passed her. But it was much faster than walking and she couldn't be seen from her parents' bedroom window. Finally, she wheeled the bike down the lane, and set out cautiously on the road to the Foster farm.

With the moon at her back, her long, distorted shadow appeared to be leading her down the road. Alone in the moonlight, the night bugs and the sounds of her bike seemed very loud to Katie. In her excitement, she found it difficult to concentrate. Although it was only a short distance, she stopped several times to listen, afraid that the moonlight would mask the approach of headlights. Her concern for avoiding detection outweighed any fear she might have had at being alone in the night.

Fortunately, the Foster house was in darkness when she arrived. To be safe, Katie walked her bike around to the far side of the barn, parking it out of sight. The view from Mr. Foster's bedroom, which she'd seen when she cleaned the room, didn't include the barn door. At least not clearly. Katie felt quite confident that she could enter the barn unseen by Mr. Foster.

Mindful of the dusty windows, Katie kept her flashlight trained on the ground. Midnight stirred in his stall.

"It's me, Midnight. It's Katie!" she whispered.

The tackroom door creaked loudly and Katie held her breath. Gary's saddle was so much bigger than hers, in tooled leather just like the one she'd hoped to win in the rodeo. It was heavy, too. Lugging it over to the horse, Katie realized that she'd need something to stand on. Midnight was a good twenty centimetres taller than Fudge.

Saddling the horse proved to be something of an ordeal. He was frisking about, presumably happy to escape his prison. Standing on a wooden crate, Katie drove her knee into the horse's stomach.

"Sorry, Midnight," she said. "I have to be sure you're not holding your breath on me."

It was a great trick of Fudge's, forcing her belly out until Katie was seated. Then suddenly the cinch would go slack and the saddle would slide to the side, toppling Katie. Stupid pet tricks, she thought.

By the time Katie and Midnight were ready, it was 11:40. She fed the horse one carrot for his patience and led him outside.

"Rats!" she exclaimed under her breath.

Katie hadn't considered how they were going to get out of the corral unseen. Two gates led out. One faced the house and led into the yard and onto the road. The other, at the end of the corral, led into the pasture. Katie had never ridden Foster's pasture, so she chose the side gate.

Midnight was impatient to leave. Katie opened the gate to the yard. Once the horse was through, she pulled it close but not closed.

Reaching up to grab the pommel, Katie hauled herself off the ground, her leg searching for the stirrup. Midnight started moving before she was seated. Clinging to the horn with one hand, Katie pulled back sharply on the reins.

"Whoa, boy!"

Her foot found the stirrup and she swung neatly into the saddle.

In a flash, Midnight was off down the road, hooves thundering in time with Katie's heart.

"Please, God, don't let anybody see me!" she prayed aloud, hoping fervently that nobody was out driving this late on a Monday night.

She planned to ride Midnight up to her secret place, but first she would let him have his head for awhile. They could always double back to the spot where the old utility track led down to the path up the hill. Katie had ridden a lot of horses in her thirteen years, but never one as big as Midnight. For a moment she feared that she wouldn't be able to hold him back. But with a quick tug on the reins, the horse slowed immediately. Katie breathed a sigh of relief and sent a silent thank you to Gary in heaven for having such a well-trained horse.

At the back of her mind, a little niggling doubt made Katie think that this might not have been such a good idea. But she was well into the adventure now. Turning the horse around, they cantered happily to the track, heading for the hills.

Katie marveled at the way the powerful horse drove forward. I bet he'd be great around the barrels, she thought, but I'll probably never find out. Higher and higher they climbed into the trees where the shadows were spooky. There were animal sounds that were ominous in the night. Katie shuddered.

Even with the moon's illumination, the ground appeared flatter than normal, forcing Katie to rely on her daylight memories of the route. The tree roots that normally stood out prominently in the path looked flat against the earth. She hoped that Midnight's night vision was better than hers.

Despite the cool air, Midnight was getting lathered.

"Almost there, boy," Katie said.

Moments later they reached the plateau, silver in the moonlight. Katie slipped down to give Midnight his treats. She wondered why horses liked carrots so much, considering how unlikely it was that they could dig them up for themselves. Apples fell on the ground and were easy to find, but carrots … it was one of those animal mysteries, like why cats, who hate water, love fish.

Those were the sorts of things that Katie liked to think about. Like why boys, especially brothers, got all the breaks. Why boys got to barbecue and girls had to bake. Why her riding shirt had goofy little frills and her brothers' didn't. Or why her clothes had flowers, or … Katie stopped herself. She realized that she was getting angry, and it was too special a night to be wasted playing the "why" game.

Instead, she played "what if," and dreamed. What if she told Mr. Foster a really funny joke and he laughed so much that he gave her Midnight to ride in the rodeo? She laughed hard at the ridiculous idea. But she was going to find a joke to tell him, just so that she could say that she had made cranky Mr. Foster laugh. Nobody would believe her so she'd have to get Paul to be her witness.

The next time she looked at the luminous dial on her sports watch it was half past two in the morning.

"Oh my gosh!" she exclaimed, panicking. By the time she got back to Mr. Foster's, unsaddled the horse and got home, it would be near dawn. Dawn on a farm meant people awake and outside, and that would be a catastrophe. Katie knew full well that it was wrong to put a horse away wet, but there just wasn't going to be time to groom Midnight.

Torn between racing the horse hard all the way to Mr. Foster's and taking it easy on him, she held her impatience and the horse in check. It took a full fifteen minutes longer to get back, and she was relieved that the house was still dark. In the east she believed she could actually see light. Her training and respect for the animal wouldn't allow her to just plunk him in the stall. She wiped him, combed him and led him in a tight circle in a corner of the corral.

It was well past three o'clock when she closed the barn door. Suddenly, a door banged open at the house. Katie froze in terror.

"Who's out there?" Mr. Foster demanded.

Katie melted into the side of the barn.

"I've got a gun and I'll use it if you don't show yourself!"

Edging along the barn, Katie reached the far side where her bike was leaning. She pedaled away as though a thousand devils were chasing her.

She didn't breathe until she reached the safety of her own yard. Katie was quite certain that Mr. Foster hadn't seen her. She crept down the concrete steps to the basement door and stepped inside.

Her hand reached automatically for the light switch just to the left of the door. With a gasp, she stopped herself, going instead to her backpack for the safety of the flashlight. Shocked, Katie realized that she didn't have the backpack. She'd dropped it outside Mr. Foster's barn.

12

Busted

Too wound up to sleep, Katie's mind raced with plans to rescue her backpack. For a brief moment she considered going back immediately, cutting across the fields on foot. But she was terrified that Mr. Foster might actually shoot at her. Better, she thought, to wait until daylight and find an excuse to go over there, like delivering some eggs or something. What if Mr. Foster found the backpack by the barn door? What if he remembered seeing the red pack on her back as she rode out of his yard yesterday?

As her room brightened with early morning sunshine, Katie's mood lifted a little as she remembered her thrilling midnight ride. The night sounds had added a touch of mystery. Finally, deep in her reverie, Katie dozed off to sleep.

She awoke with a start, uncertain for a moment where she was. Remembering her dilemma, she was anxious to get going to recover her backpack. She had fallen asleep in her clothes, but they were dusty from the trail, so she quickly changed.

The family was bustling about in the kitchen, and the wonderful aroma of bacon wafted up the stairs. Katie realized that she was starving. She raced down the stairs and burst into the kitchen full of enthusiasm, only to stop dead in her tracks. On her chair at the breakfast table sat her red backpack.

She stood paralyzed behind the chair, unable to bring herself to pick up her backpack. Katie became aware of her parents' eyes on her. This could only mean one thing. Her mother must have remembered hanging the backpack on the hook by the door just before dinner last night. It took all of Katie's self-control not to run from the room. Her father broke the unbearable silence.

"Is there something you'd like to tell us, Katie?" he asked sternly.

Katie said the first thing that popped into her head.

"No."

"What were you doing at Mr. Foster's this morning?" he continued.

"I ... I ... I went to see the horse," Katie stammered. "I couldn't sleep so I just went there for a visit."

She could feel the heat in her face.

"Did you ride him?" Her father was relentless.

Katie looked at her mother for pity, but her mother looked back with concern.

"No," she lied.

"You're absolutely certain you didn't ride the horse?"

Katie was sweating now. She wanted desperately to deny it, but she couldn't look her father in the eye and say no again. Instead she hung her head, mumbling her admission.

Her mother sat down in the chair beside Katie.

"Why, Katie?" she asked softly.

Before Katie had a chance to answer, her father cut in.

"That was a dangerous, foolish thing to do!" he said, angrily. "He told you to stay away from that horse, but you just couldn't leave it alone. What the devil has gotten into you, Katie Mavrinac?"

"I just wanted to ride him, even just once," Katie mumbled miserably.

"We've got horses of our own for you to ride," her father snapped.

Her father's remark fanned the flame of indignation in Katie. If there had been enough horses to go around, none of this would have happened.

"We do not!" Katie retorted, her voice unexpectedly loud. She pointed at her father. "You took my horse away from me!"

The emotion welled up in her, nearly making her choke. Rather than let her parents see her cry, Katie marched with dignity to the door. Without a backward look, she walked out into the sunshine. For a moment, she stood in the yard, looking around. Spying the ATV parked beside the fuel pump, Katie ran to it.

Luckily, the key was in the ignition. She looped the kill cord around her wrist, settled onto the padded seat and started the machine. Katie was out of the yard like a shot, bouncing down the road toward the back pasture and the hills beyond. She would take the ATV to the base of the hills, and go the rest of the way on foot, up to her secret place.

Too many thoughts crowded her head. Katie realized that taking Midnight without permission was wrong. She also realized that walking out of the argument with her parents wasn't such a bright idea either. But resentment was boiling at the bottom of her emotions, stirring everything up. Deep in thought, she neglected to note that the fuel gauge was on empty.

Suddenly, the vehicle stopped without a cough or sputter to warn her. Katie was left sitting out in the middle of the green pasture, going nowhere fast.

Without the steady hum of the ATV's engine, Katie heard the unmistakable sound of hoofbeats. She turned around to see her father coming up fast behind her.

"Might as well face the music," Katie said out loud, as if the ATV could hear her.

Ranger slowed to a halt a short distance away. Her father dismounted and walked to Katie, leading the horse behind him. He tied the animal to the vehicle, put his hand briefly on Katie's shoulder, then sat on the grass, looking up at her.

"So, Kate," he said, "I guess you're pretty mad at me, huh?"

Immediately, Katie was taken aback. She didn't know how to respond, but she tried anyway.

"Um, yeah, maybe a little."

Her father laughed. "A little? I think it's more like a lot."

"Yeah, maybe."

It felt really odd looking down at her dad like that, but Katie made no move to join him on the ground.

"I'm prepared to sit here all day, Katie, just as long as we reach an understanding at some point. Now, I believe you said I'm responsible for taking your horse away. Right?"

"Well, you did," Katie replied.

"I thought you understood the circumstances. If you had spoken up at the time, told us how strongly you felt then, I never would have allowed it," her dad said earnestly.

Katie was surprised by her father's remark. She struggled to find the right words to convey her confusion.

"I never felt like I had a choice. You expected it, you and John and everybody." Katie's indignation rose. "Nobody asked me how I felt."

Fingers drumming on the ground, her dad thought about this for a moment before answering.

"Kate, you're right. Nobody asked. But if you wait to be asked how you feel every time, I guarantee you, you won't need that many answers. I'm not saying it's right, but that's the way it is."

Now it was Katie's turn to think. Idly, she turned the steering wheel back and forth, the tires squelching on the grass.

"So I can have my horse back?"

"If that's what you want, you've got it," her Dad replied. "So this business with Mr. Foster and Midnight, was it all because you were mad at us?"

"I guess," Katie thought about her answer, which didn't really cover all of it. "You don't take me seriously. I really, really want to race in the rodeo, to win the saddle. You didn't do enough to help me."

"If you want a new saddle, Katie, we'll get you one," her dad said, missing the point.

"I want to ride so I can *win* the saddle!" Katie exclaimed, exasperated.

It seemed to her that her father was surprised by her competitiveness.

"Dad, you treat me differently than you treat the boys, and it makes me feel less important than they are."

Her father whistled softly.

"Oh, boy," he said.

A long pause followed, and then he cleared his throat.

"Katie, I have to admit you're half right. I do treat boys and girls differently. That's the way I was brought up, and I find it pretty hard to be … non-sexist, or whatever the right term is. It's hard to change a lifetime of values. But I don't mean to be unkind or unfair."

Katie nodded her head. Her father went on.

"As far as the other thing you mentioned, about being less important, nothing could be farther from the truth. At least not in my eyes. I hope you can believe that, Katie, because it's true."

"So why do you always do stuff with them, but not with me?" Katie asked.

"The same reason your mom does things with you that she doesn't do with the boys. It's what we're used to. But it doesn't have to be that way. Anytime you want to join in, you just speak up."

"You could ask me," Katie said reasonably.

Her dad laughed heartily.

"You've got me there, kiddo. So here's the deal. You speak up for yourself when you think you're getting the short end, and I'll start treating you like — " he hesitated, smiling broadly. "I was going to say like one of the boys, but that's not right either is it?"

"Nope," Katie said. "But I think I know what you mean. You can just treat us all the same. How's that?"

"Done!" he agreed.

Katie's dad stood up and embraced her warmly. She hugged him back, too pleased to speak.

"You have two choices, Kate. One, I get back on my horse, ride home and get some gas for that machine. Or *you* get on my horse, ride home and get some gas. What do you say?"

Katie found her voice. "I'll ride!"

She sprung into the saddle, without even adjusting the stirrups. Her dad untied Ranger and handed Katie the reins.

"Just once around the pasture, then home and straight back here, okay? I've got work to do," he shouted after her.

On her ride home, Katie realized that she had two other choices concerning her horse. First, she could take Fudge back from John, ride in the rodeo and maybe win the saddle. Or, she could let John keep Fudge for the rodeo and sit it out. In the first case, Katie would get what she wanted. But John would lose the chance of being undefeated as best all-round rider in his junior career. It was in Katie's power to give him that chance.

By the time she returned to her father with the gas, she had made up her mind.

"Dad," she began. "I've been thinking, and I've decided that John should ride Fudge in the rodeo."

"That's very generous of you, Katie. But you don't have to. I just wish we had another horse around here that would be as competitive as Fudge," he replied. "Too bad old Ranger here is past it," he laughed, playfully putting his hands over his horse's ears.

Katie started the ATV as her father jumped into the saddle.

Over the hum of the engine, he said, "I don't want to spoil your day, Katie, but don't forget you owe Mr. Foster a visit."

13

Getting Past "No"

At least, Katie thought, Mr. Foster's not going to shoot me in broad daylight. She tried to cajole Paul into coming with her, but to no avail. So she pointed the ATV in the direction of Mr. Foster's farm, ready to face the music.

On the road, she waved at a truck towing a horse trailer, although she wasn't sure who it was. She was just being friendly. The trip took only a few minutes. Katie wondered why she hadn't walked, to delay the inevitable.

Her knock on the screen door went unanswered, although the house was open. She opened the door, peeked around into the living room and called out for Mr. Foster. Puzzled, she went back to stand by the ATV in the yard. Then she noticed that both the paddock gate and the barn door were wide open. Concerned, Katie ran into the barn.

To her horror, Midnight's stall was open and empty. She gasped aloud. Oh my gosh, she thought, did I do this? A chair or something scraped the ground in the tack room. However unlikely it was, Katie hoped that Midnight was in there. Instead, she found Mr. Foster, beside the wooden saw horse that held Gary's saddle.

"Mr. Foster!" she cried. "What happened to Midnight? Did he get away?"

"All that fuss over a horse," he said. "I told Gary that a black horse is bad luck, like a black cat. Wouldn't have one myself."

Mr. Foster's tone and the talk about bad luck frightened Katie. She was afraid for Midnight.

"What happened, Mr. Foster? Where's Midnight?"

"Where's Midnight? Gone! You wanted him out of here. Well, you got your wish. Half of it anyway. He's gone. Sold to Charlie. Now everybody can just stop pestering me about that horse."

Katie's relief that nothing bad had happened to Midnight Run was mixed with sadness. She had become attached to him. Now not only would she not be able to ride him in the rodeo, but she probably wouldn't even see him again. The weight of her regret lent her apology to Mr. Foster that much more sincerity.

At supper that night, Katie told her parents what Mr. Foster had done. Her mother listened to Katie recount her conversation with Mr. Foster.

When she was done, Katie's mom said thoughtfully, "You know something? If it weren't for you, Katie, Mr. Foster might have kept Midnight locked up in that barn forever and Charlie would never have gotten his hands on him."

Katie jumped out of her chair, knocking it to the floor.

"Dad," she exclaimed, "you've got to drive me over to Charlie's place! Right now!"

"Whoa, Katie," her dad said. "What gives?"

"Like Mom said, if it weren't for me, Charlie never would have gotten Midnight from Mr. Foster. I did him a favour. And now I'm going to ask him for one back."

Katie's mom interjected, "I think that's fair, Phil. But why don't we finish dinner first?"

After dinner, they drove to the Wilder spread in the truck. Katie ran the words over and over in her mind. She was going to ask Charlie if she could borrow his horse. She was nervous by the time they arrived at the ranch and parked in front of the small white bungalow where Charlie lived. Charlie's father was sitting in a chair on the porch of the big house next door. He walked down off the porch to greet them.

"Evening, Bob. We're looking for Charlie," Katie's dad said to the older man.

"He's in the big barn. Go right on in," Bob replied.

With that, he turned and went back to his chair on the porch. Katie ran ahead of her dad, hoping she would see Midnight again. Inside the barn, she followed the sound of whistling to a tackroom, where Charlie was just hanging up a bridle.

Charlie Wilder was a solidly built young man with close-cropped blond hair. When he smiled, which he did a lot, his blue eyes would all but disappear.

"Hi Charlie, do you remember me, Katie Mavrinac?" she said in greeting.

"I sure do. How are you, Katie? What brings you out here?" Charlie replied.

Now at the moment of truth, Katie got stage fright. She looked around for the moral support of her dad. Charlie was looking expectantly at her. Finally, her dad called out, looking for her.

"Down here, Dad," she shouted, smiling lamely at Charlie.

Mr. Mavrinac joined them in the tackroom and the two men exchanged greetings.

"So Phil, what can I do for you?" Charlie was clearly curious to know why they were there.

"Nothing for me," Katie's dad answered. "But Katie has something to ask you."

This was it. Katie cleared her throat and launched into her pitch. When she was finished, Charlie was laughing out loud.

"Let me get this straight," he said. "You pestered old man Foster about Midnight until he couldn't take it anymore. So he sold the horse to me, just to stop you. Is that about right?"

Katie was pretty embarrassed that Charlie was laughing at her, so instead of answering, she just nodded her head. Her dad answered for her.

"That's pretty much the way it happened Charlie," he said.

"Brilliant!" Charlie exclaimed, laughing harder still.

Katie cheered up quite a bit at his remark.

"So, um, Charlie? Would it be okay if I borrowed Midnight for the Heritage Days Jamboree and Rodeo?" she said hesitantly.

Charlie winked at Katie's dad. "Fair's fair, eh?"

"I think that means yes, Katie," her dad said.

"Oh, thank you!" Katie jumped up and down with excitement.

"I've been trying to get my hands on that horse for months. Guess I just should have hired Katie to arrange it sooner." Charlie started laughing again.

Katie found Midnight roaming the horse pasture. He looked happy to be free at last.

"Midnight, come here, boy!" Katie called to him. "I've got something to tell you!"

When she caught up to him, Midnight started nudging her pockets looking for treats. Katie laughed, despite having empty pockets.

"You and I are going to win that barrel race, okay?" She tugged on Midnight's muzzle to make him nod in agreement with her. "But first we have to practice. Dad's going to bring me over here everyday until the rodeo. We're going to be so good!"

For the first time in a long time, Katie was looking forward to the rodeo.

14

Around and Around She Goes

Katie's mom was putting the finishing touches on her new red, black and white shirt for the rodeo the next day.

"Stop fidgeting, just for a minute," she said.

With Katie standing still for a change, her mother took advantage of the moment. "Katie, honey, there's something I want to talk to you about," she began.

Oh, oh, thought Katie, what have I done now? But her mother's face was kind, not stern or threatening. Katie relaxed a bit.

"I put that idea in your head about Charlie owing you a favour. Now everyone thinks it's funny that you annoyed poor Mr. Foster until he got rid of the horse. Just because it worked out well for Charlie, and you got a horse to ride in the bargain doesn't make your behaviour entirely acceptable. Do you understand that, Katie?"

"What about that squeaky wheel thing?" Katie asked. "Isn't it sort of like that?"

Her mother smiled. "Let me put it this way. It was perfectly okay for you to ask Mr. Foster if you could borrow the horse. But, when he said no, you should have accepted it. When he told you to stay away from the horse, you should have done so. I'm not saying Mr. Foster should have treated

Midnight the way he did, but it was his horse, and that was his right."

Katie looked at her mother seriously. "Life's pretty complicated, isn't it, Mom?"

"It sure is, Katie," she replied. "But you'll do just fine. Now give me that shirt. You've got a big race tomorrow."

By the next day, the town was transformed. Heritage Days banners were stretched across the main street and flying from every available pole. It was a festive time, and everyone was in the spirit. The line of trucks towing horse trailers stretched for miles, or so it seemed to Katie who was anxious to get parked and settled.

In the hour before her first event, Katie put in a shift at the 4-H barbecue stand. When Tracy arrived for her shift, Katie was with the girls, handling condiments and baked goods.

Tracy gave Katie a puzzled look. "Weren't you supposed to be working the barbeque pit?" she asked.

Katie and the other girls laughed out loud. "I did. And you know what? It was hot and boring and smoke gets in your eyes all the time. Plus you end up smelling like smoke and burned meat."

"Aren't you afraid the guys will think you couldn't handle it?" Tracy said.

"Nah," Katie answered, looking over at the barbecues where her brother was flipping steaks. "John begged me to switch. I made him promise to stop calling me Kate the Snake."

"Brilliant!" exclaimed Tracy.

Their conversation was interrupted by Katie's mom, who had come to collect Katie and John for their first event, the pole-bend. It was one of the few events in which boys and girls competed together, but there was still a separate prize for each.

The rodeo was held outside on the land beside the feed co-op. The ring was normally used for outdoor auctions and during the rodeo extra bleachers were brought in for the spectators. Colourful bunting lined the ring, along with the occasional advertising banner. The judges and official timer sat on a platform high above the crowd. The livestock pens beside the co-op building were filled with prize livestock to be judged.

On the opposite side of the ring, rows of long rails were staked into the ground. Here, the competitors could tie their horses while they waited their turns.

John, as the former boys' winner, would ride last. Katie was near the middle of the pack of fifty kids, which was where she'd finished last year.

Katie swung into the saddle. Her brother looked over enviously.

"Kate," he said, "Don't you go beating your big brother, Okay?"

She detected a note of real worry in John's voice and it made her sit up taller in the saddle. Imagine being a threat to John, the undefeated junior cowboy. The thought made Katie swell with pride.

"Watch me!" she teased.

At the end of the arena was a big, portable, electric scoreboard sign that posted each rider's time, and the time to beat. John, who managed to remember every time he'd ever posted in any event, would say "nope," "whew," "that was close," or something like it as each rider completed the circuit.

Katie's turn arrived. She steered Midnight to the starting mark outside the arena gates. The official signalled her start and Katie spurred her horse through the timing gate. A flag on a wooden pole was stuck in a barrel just inside the arena. As Katie and Midnight passed to the right of the barrel, Katie leaned to her left and snatched up the pole. Careful to keep it away from the horse's legs, she dug her knees into Midnight's sides, driving him hard toward the barrel at the other end. It was a sharp turn at the barrel, reversing direction, and Midnight leaned hard into it allowing Katie to plant the pole in the end barrel securely.

Six poles stood on either side of the arena, forming four gates. Horse and rider had to pass cleanly through each gate, going up one side and down the other. Midnight changed gears smoothly, slowing as they entered the first gate. Katie shifted her weight with the horse, leaning first one way then the other, four times until each of the gates on one side had been successfully cleared. Crossing to the other side, Katie kept up a constant flow of chatter, counting down the gates.

On the last gate of the downside, Midnight shifted too soon. Katie was suddenly out of sync with his motion. For a scary moment, she felt herself come unglued from the saddle. She had only a second to recover, as they neared the end. Katie found herself leaning the wrong way as they passed beside the flag. Flinging her weight across the horse, she caught the fabric of the flag and dragged the pole out of the barrel. Midnight was thundering home as he had been trained to do.

Katie had to do something desperate in the scant seconds before she had to plant the pole in the top barrel. Fearful of tangling the pole in her horse's flying feet, she flicked it forward by the flag end, and by some miracle, was able to clasp the bamboo pole in time to jam it into the barrel.

In a flash, horse and rider were through the timing gate and into the run-off area.

She could see Paul jumping up and down, pointing to the scoreboard. The smile on his face told her all she needed to know. When Midnight was brought to a halt, Katie swung around to look. Her elapsed time and the time to beat were the same. She was winning!

When Katie located John, she shouted to him, "How close? How close?"

"Too close," came his reply.

Now came the really hard part. Katie had to watch and see how long her time would stand. It was extremely difficult to do, so Katie chose to wait with John instead of heading to the stands for a better look. Her eyes were drawn like magnets to the big, electric signboard, where every minute that ticked by seemed like it was taking a year off Katie's life.

I asked for this, she thought, and it's ten times worse than worrying about finding a horse to ride! When the race official called John on deck, Katie snapped out of her trance with a start. Last rider and her time still stood. It was down to Katie and her own brother. What should she say? Brother and sister looked at each other seriously until they both burst out laughing. Without a word between them and with mixed emotions, Katie watched John roar into the arena to the enthusiastic applause of the crowd.

Katie's mom, dad and brother Paul materialized around her. Together they cheered John on. Watching him work the course, Katie wondered if she had looked so in control, or so relaxed. John was in the home stretch, the clock counter running faster than her eye could register. Then it stopped. One tiny tenth of a second faster than Katie.

Her dad and mom squashed her in a hug between them.

"First and second! Katie, do know what that means?" her dad exclaimed proudly.

Sure, Katie thought, it means I didn't win. But her father went on talking without waiting for her to answer.

"You went from twenty-seventh to second in one year! That's amazing! John never did that."

When Katie finally found her voice, it was to congratulate her big brother who, after two events, was well on his way to retaining his title as best all-round rider for the fifth year in a row.

Katie ran to get Midnight and together with John on Fudge, they accepted their ribbons.

As they rode out of the arena the announcer said, "The next event is the Girls' Barrel Race. All competitors please proceed to the arena."

All of the girls who had competed in the pole-bend, plus a few who hadn't, lined up to receive their numbers. Katie's place in the pole-bend gave her second-to-last spot. For this race, there would be two heats for best combined time. Before she went back to her horse, Katie paused to admire the prized saddle.

"Good luck, Katie," Felicity Fullerton said. Katie hadn't noticed her standing there.

Each of the first twelve riders knocked a barrel over. That was a three second penalty. In a race that takes less than thirty seconds to run on a slow horse, it is a big hit. Katie started to wonder if the barrels had round bottoms. But as the more experienced riders made their runs, there were fewer mishaps. By the time Katie's turn came, the time to beat was 19.69 seconds.

"Okay, Midnight," she said to her horse. "We don't have to win the heat to win the event. But it would be nice."

Then they were off. Her hat was blown away almost immediately. Her concentration flickered for a second, but Midnight roared on like a big, black train, rounding the first barrel smoothly. The second barrel was no less smooth and Katie dug in, flicking the loose ends of the reins back and forth over the animal's rump. Midnight brushed the barrel in the tight u-turn at the end and it wobbled slightly. Katie held her breath. Without knowing if the barrel was up or down, they tore for the finish.

Katie checked the end barrel, before she checked the score board. It was still standing and, for the second time today, her time was the best, at 19.66 seconds. Only one rider remained, reigning girls' champion Loretta Pavlik. Loretta was seventeen and, like John, was competing as a junior for the last time. In 19.63 seconds Katie found herself in second place, also for the second time today.

It would all be over in less than fifteen minutes. The family gathered around Katie and Midnight, fussing, encouraging and lending support. As the second heat got underway, John made a surprising suggestion.

"Dad, Mom, why don't you go into the stands? I'll stay here with Katie. Don't you want a front row seat for her winning ride?" he said.

"Katie?" her mom said, looking at her with concern. "Would you mind? I'd really like to watch you from the stands."

"You go on," Katie replied. "I'll be fine. With John," she added.

"Good luck, kiddo," her dad said.

Waving after them, Katie felt a rush of pride. They were a pretty good family after all.

"Kate," John said. "Concentrate, now. You cut the bottom turn tight because you went at it too fast. He'll run like the wind whether you drive him or not, so concentrate on control, not speed. Believe me, kid, you've got speed to burn."

Her turn was coming up, and Katie was relieved to see that the best time in this heat was 19.75 seconds. She leaned over to pat Midnight on the neck and offer some encouraging words.

John led them into position as the announcer said, "Next up is our dark horse, Katie Mavrinac and Midnight Run."

Katie's heart beat in time with the applause. She kept her eyes straight ahead, not wanting to know where the family was seated.

"Concentrate, concentrate," she said, over and over.

The flag was down. Midnight jolted forward. Instantly the world around Katie grew silent. She heard only the sounds of her own fast breathing, the blood pounding in her head and the snorting breath of her horse.

In Katie's eyes, the first barrel, on the right side, appeared to be pulsing. She leaned low over Midnight's neck, anticipating the first turn. Katie let Midnight lead into the top of the figure-eight. She urged him across the arena to the next barrel.

Midnight's shifts were as smooth as silk. Katie felt confident and in control as the big horse executed his turns perfectly. Katie could tell that this figure-eight was even tighter than the previous one.

Bearing down on the end barrel, Katie felt the hair rise on her arms. She steered Midnight a fraction farther to the left of the end barrel. Too far and she'd lose time, not far enough and they could hit the barrel or, worse, knock it over completely.

They were on it. Midnight made an impossibly tight turn. Katie imagined she could feel the barrel brush her leg as they passed it on the downslide. She allowed herself a quick glance to see that the barrel was rock still. Midnight needed no additional urging to the finish. Heart pumping, head down, body low, Katie and Midnight swept past the timing gate, confident that she had given it her best shot.

The shouting in the stands confirmed it, even before she saw her time of 19.59 seconds. Loretta and Katie nodded to each other as Katie passed by. Loretta was already into her run when Katie turned to watch. This time, she watched Loretta's ride instead of the clock. In her head, she was tracing her own path, matching the turns. Wide here, tight there.

John murmured beside her, "Too slow, too fast, too slow."

Loretta's time in the second heat was exactly the same as the first: 19.63 seconds for a combined time of 39.26 seconds. John, the human computer, was a fraction ahead of the scoreboard, pulling Katie out of the saddle into a huge bearhug.

"You won!" he screamed, "39.25 seconds. You won! You won!"

Still clutching Katie, with her feet dangling above the ground, John managed to jump up and down with glee.

Her family swarmed Katie, jumping and whooping until a race official came to find her. They were waiting for Katie in the arena to award the prizes.

Eight hands and arms pushed Katie back into the saddle. John jammed Katie's hat onto her head. "Get in there, Kate," her dad said. "Mary, have you got the camera ready?"

John slapped Midnight's rump and Katie headed back into the arena. A cheer arose from the spectators. Katie had never experienced such acclaim. It was overwhelming. She waved her hat at the crowd, blushing furiously. In the centre of the arena stood the judges and Felicity Fullerton. The prize saddle was on a sawhorse at her side. Katie found it difficult to take her eyes off of it.

She felt kind of silly sitting up there on her horse while the judges pinned the blue ribbon on Midnight's bridle. Her mother moved around the group, happily snapping pictures.

"Congratulations, Katie," Felicity Fullerton said warmly. "You had two great runs."

"Thank you," Katie croaked, nearly overcome with joy.

"Are you sorry you have to give Midnight back to Charlie?" Felicity asked.

"Yes, um, I mean, no. I already have a horse," Katie replied. It was complicated, how Katie really felt about it. She didn't want to think about giving Midnight back right now. "A deal's a deal," she said finally. Felicity smiled and reached for the saddle on the stand.

"This saddle's going to look mighty nice on Fudge, isn't it, Katie?"

"Oh yes!" Katie beamed, "It's perfect."

The crowd was on their feet, cheering. An uncharacteristically tongue-tied Katie murmured her thanks to Felicity and the judges and rode out of the ring, clutching the saddle.

She found Charlie Wilder standing with her family. She handed the saddle down to her father and offered the blue ribbon to Charlie, as thanks for the loan of Midnight. Good-natured Charlie laughed, declining the offer.

"There is something you can do for me, Katie," he said. "I've got my eye on Bob Cudmore's tractor. Maybe you could ask him if you can ride it in the tractor pull. Then he'll sell it to me, just to … "

Katie cut him off. "No way!"

While her family re-lived the highlights of the day, Katie slid out of the saddle. Rummaging in her mother's carry-all, she found the bag she'd put in there earlier.

Katie stroked Midnight's nose with one hand and fed him apples with the other. "I'll never forget you, big fella," she said. "Thanks for the ride of my life."